HIDDEN:

The Memory Thief

By Ashley Williams

ASIN: B01LWVYGJ9

KDP ISBN: 9781520253930

HIDDEN:

The Memory Thief

TABLE OF CONTENTS

THE BEGINNING

This was the darkest night of the year. The clouds had overcast the twinkling stars and the scenery was draped with a velvety darkness. On this night, the shadows roamed freely, but there was no fear; everything was calm. The familiar night sounds began to stir and the light of the moon could be seen peeking through the clouds. As the cadence of the night slowed to a low murmur, the scene fell silent.

A short distance away, the silhouette of three figures could be seen approaching. The stillness of the night was not disturbed by their presence. In fact, it seemed as if they were akin to the nightfall. With each step forward, the brightness of the moon dimmed and in a matter of moments three women stood in the middle of the formerly deserted field.

"What if they find us?" Marlena's voice quivered. Her attempt at masking the fear in her voice was unsuccessful. She prided herself on being strong for her two younger sisters, but tonight her strength alone could not protect them. Her hair hung just below her waist and blended in perfectly with the blanket of darkness that had settled amongst them. The light from the moon danced and disappeared against her rich, brown pigmented skin as she composed herself.

Marlena turned to Venus awaiting a response. Though her sister stood no taller than a whooping crane, her spirit was that of a giant. The juxtaposition of her deep olive skin and the copper curls framing her face was the essence of her beauty. She nervously twirled a curl around her finger before speaking.

"They won't..." Venus hesitated, "...if we do this right."

Safina huffed, "We will only know that we have not failed if they do not come." Her voice filled with concern, "I have never heard of anyone invoking an infinite cloaking spell."

Safina was the youngest of the three but towered over her sisters; her height correlated with her unmatched wisdom. Her unblemished skin was a deep brown with red undertones like the trunks of the paperbark maples surrounding them.

Marlena mustered a weak smile, "We won't be the first and we won't be the last. Plus, we have every reason to make it work."

No one spoke as the women's eyes lingered on their cargo. Each child was less than a day old. At first glance, these infants could be mistaken for ordinary, but upon closer inspection, you would notice the cosmos in their eyes. These were the promised ones. And as promised, they were filled with an energy that resonated through every dimension. The women formed a circle and linked their arms. The subtle differences in their skin tones blended like the unique shades of wool that can be found in a beautiful handwoven blanket. But unlike a blanket, their arms did not offer comfort on this night.

"Keep them covered," Marlena commanded, shielding the newborns from the glimmer of moonlight. "We have to concentrate! One chance," she stated lifting her index finger, "That is all we have."

The women's faces remained somber. With interlocked arms, they closed their eyes and channeled their energy. They needed to become one with their surroundings. The night stood still, but the energy around the group sent ripples through the atmosphere. Silence engulfed them until they were one with the field; no more noticeable than the shadows cast by the trees. Venus was the first to break the silence.

"We call upon the night to cloak this dimension from now until eternity! My sisters, we must think the thoughts of shadows," Venus shouted!

The women began to sway back and forth, allowing their essence to evaporate into the night.

Safina's voice was barely above a whisper, "Let the breeze flow through your veins!"

The women continued to chant as an icy cold entered their circle.

"Force the energy behind the Wall," said Marlena.

The temperature inside of the circle continued to drop. The ground beneath them began to shake, but the women were unbothered.

"Seal the Wall!" the women chanted, "Seal the Wall! Seal the Wall! Seal the Wall!"

Silence.

At this moment, the Earth stood still. The icy cold disappeared, and the ground was stable. The women dropped their arms and stared into the faces of the children with remorse.

"The seal is not strong enough. I can still feel them all pushing against it, fighting to escape," Safina stammered.

"I know. I can feel them too," Marlena bent down to rummage through their belongings, "Did you bring them?" she questioned Venus.

Venus hesitated, but obediently removed the Emerald daggers from the satchel on her hip, "I didn't want it to come to this."

"We have to seal the Wall or all of this was for nothing!" Marlena agonized as her eyes filled with tears.

Her words rang true. Sacrifices always had to be made for the greater good. Each woman held a blade in one hand and a baby in the other.

"May the blood of the Innocents seal the Wall and protect this dimension," the women chanted in unison.

The daggers sliced through the air with ease. The soft flesh of the infants was no match for the serrated blades. Upon contact, the barrier of skin gave way to the pressure, drenching the women in blood. Again, the ground beneath them began to quiver, preparing to devour the Wall forever.

The deed was done.

"I don't feel them anymore," Safina reassured.

The other two sisters simply nodded in agreeance. Taking a deep breath, the three women finalized the spell:

"May the blood of the Innocents seal the Wall and protect this dimension," the women roared! "Seal the Wall! Seal the Wall! Seal the Wall!"

Their voices trailed off into the darkness taking bits and pieces of who they were with them until there was nothing left of them but vapor. The dry ground was now soaked with the blood of the Innocents. Once completely saturated, the Seal would be complete.

The women vanished into the night; the regret had not had the chance to seep into their bones before they had left those bones behind. Fear encouraged them to move quickly, but desperation required it. The essence of the Innocents was fleeting, and they needed to find new hosts for the children, quickly.

Safina broke the silence, "We have to split them up."

"What good is splitting them up?" Marlena questioned, "Their fate is together, and they will always find their way back to one another. Nothing we try will change that."

Marlena's words were sobering, but the women knew that the Innocents stood a greater chance of survival if they remained apart.

"If we place them in different bloodlines there is a lower chance that their paths will cross," Venus suggested.

Safina nodded in agreement and smashed the emerald daggers to pieces. She undressed and lay her bloody garments over the fragments of the blade, "May the Innocents rest in the shadows."

Venus slipped out of her soiled garb and lay it next to Safina's. "May their light be forever dimmed," she added.

Marlena removed her shoulders from the gown and let the blood-stained frock slink to the ground. Placing her gown alongside the others she whispered, "May the blood of their keepers never mix."

The three women watched as the essence of the Innocents dispersed and vanished over the horizon in search of their new vessels.

As the sisters continued to fade into obscurity, they uttered their last words, "May they stay forever hidden."

For years, the Seal remained intact. The Earth had sopped up the blood of the Innocents, and the Dimension was cloaked.

But, nothing lasts forever.

One year, as the seasons changed, the Wall began to crack.

They were coming.

CHAPTER 1: THE MEMORY THIEF

It slithered through a crack in the Wall.

This was the first time the Creature had ever been to this dimension. Though he was not bound by the constraints of time and space, the Wall had kept him a prisoner. When fully upright, he stood about a foot above an average headstone. The Creature shared many similarities with the human form but its hunched back, grotesquely protruding abdomen, and amphibious, soot-colored skin linked it to a much darker lineage; the Mares. Mares, commonly seen in German folklore, are most known for tormenting sleeping victims. While similar in appearance, this tormentor preferred to steal dreams rather than haunt them.

Slithering had become its preferred method of locomotion --it was the easiest way to get around unseen. Before escaping the Wall, the Creature had learned that regardless of the dimension, the dominant species always had their heads so far in the clouds they never even bothered to look down. Lack of awareness had always worked to his advantage --an unsuspecting victim was a much easier victim.

Planting his feet firmly in the ground, the Creature began to pant. The temperature of this dimension was much different from the frigid darkness that existed behind the Wall. He crept carefully over the rocky soil on his hands and knees to avoid the rays from the sun. The shade of the paperbark maples now served a dual purpose: blocking the heat that his body was not yet accustomed to, and masking his presence as he explored this new-found land.

Once his body adjusted to the new environment, the idea that he was free took root. Edging ever so carefully towards the portal from which he had escaped, the abomination spat from the gaping hole that embodied much of its face. The feeling of freedom empowered him but when the fear of being sucked back into the darkness overcame him, the Creature immediately scurried away. During this retreat, he couldn't help but notice the faint scent of a pheromone he had grown to crave: power.

Now seated in a crouched position in the shade, he grabbed a fistful of the arid ground beneath him. Without hesitation, he threw his head back and a large tongue emerged from its mouth. The bulbous appendage appeared as rough as sandpaper, but the Creature licked its hand with ease. Even when his hand was saturated with saliva, it was clear that he was not satisfied. Dragging its tongue along the ground, searching for the trail from which that last taste originated, a slight buzzing noise began to resonate from its body:

BUZZZZZZZ BUZZ BUZZ BUZZZZZZZ

The internal buzzing caused the body of the recently escaped monster to vibrate. The vibrations were a result of the churning of volatile memories attempting to escape from his hold. For many years, this Creature had stolen the memories of the unsuspecting, without considering that not all memories are good memories. Having spent his young life alone, he had never been warned of the unspoken power that the memories of the damned possessed. Unfortunately for him, it was too late. Though he considered himself the Prince of the Night, he was nothing more than the twilight's slave.

He was now addicted to the thrill of transformation. By engulfing the memories of his victims, he was able to take their physical form and walk amongst the inhabitants of whichever dimension he stumbled upon. More times than not, however, the Creature could not stop at just stealing the memories. Living in the shadows for so long coupled with the influence of the damned memories awakened a dark bloodlust inside of him. He was cursed with an insatiable taste for souls. Each soul he devoured became a part of him, forever trapped in his internal purgatory. No matter how he tried to fight the urge, his body craved the writhing within. And honestly, after years of solitude, he welcomed the company.

The Creature scampered about searching the immediate area to find the one who tasted of such great power but was unsuccessful. Whatever or whomever the monstrosity had sampled seemed to stir the spirits living within its small frame. The spirits all agreed—they wanted that power to join them. What could only be considered a smile, crept onto the Creature's face and the low buzzing continued.

At last, The Memory Thief was free.

CHAPTER 2: THE CALL

"How boring is this, Amina?" Tiana muttered as she passed the wine bottle in my direction.

A small jolt of electricity shot through my hand the instance I grabbed the bottle.

"Ouch," I winced in pain, "What did you do? Drag your feet across the carpet before handing it to me?"

Tiana shook her head, "Don't blame me. That was definitely your fault."

Wine bottle in hand, I assessed our current situation. Although this wasn't my favorite thing to do on a Friday night, a girl's night sure beat a night of binge-watching the most recent season of *Orange is the New Black*...for the third time in a row, alone. Plus, I was wearing my comfy yoga pants and nothing is ever wrong in comfy yoga pants. *Not that it matters that I've never actually been to a yoga class.*

"Well T, what would you rather we do?" I asked, filling my wine glass to the rim.

A sly grin spread across her face, "I have a brilliant idea."

I slowly sipped my umpteenth glass of red wine, fully anticipating the worst.

"I need you to keep an open mind," she began, "We haven't done this in years, but I think that it could be really fun."

"Spit it out already," I urged.

"Let's make prank calls!" she proposed. The look on her face was that of excitement and pride as if she had just come up with the most original and exhilarating idea in history.

I didn't feel the need to justify her suggestion with a response. I simply rolled my eyes and continued to sip my wine.

"What? Do you have a better idea?" she scowled.

I'll assume my face didn't hide my lack of enthusiasm for her plan.

As the last drop of wine passed my lips, I realized that I didn't have a better idea…but I did have a valid objection, "We are entirely too old to prank call anyone. Plus, it's the 21st century, T!"

"And?" she pushed.

"Everyone has caller ID," I gently reminded her.

"So we don't call from our actual phone numbers," she responded matter-of-factly while thumbing through her cellphone. After a few seconds of scrolling, she flipped her screen in my direction, "We can just download an app that can disguise our number. Didn't you know that smarty pants?"

I should have known she would already have an answer for any objection I could possibly come up with. When Tiana came up with a plan, there was no stopping her.

"I really just wanted to have a relaxing evening with my best friend. It's been a long week and I don't want to get into any trouble tonight, T," I whined.

She sighed, "You can't be a scaredy-cat all of your life, Amina. What's the worst that could happen?"

To rid myself of the "friend who's always scared" image, I conceded. So now here we are…. two 26-year-old women prank calling people on a Friday night. And the award for the lamest Friday night goes to….

"Is your refrigerator running?" Tiana huffed into the phone. Her prank calling voice was a mix between a really terrible British accent and a chain smoker. Tiana placed the call on speakerphone.

The voice on the other end of the phone was not amused, "Are you kidding me? How old are you?"

Not one to be easily thwarted, Tiana quickly came up with a counter, "I'm sorry, I don't understand. This is maintenance. We got a call that you were having some electrical issues in your building, so I wanted to reach out to ensure your groceries weren't in danger of spoiling."

I had to give it to her: The girl was quick on her feet.

I'm not sure if the prankee decided to play along or if they had somehow managed to hear the sincerity in her terrible prank calling voice, but either the way they took the bait.

"Oh, I apologize! Let me check." Seconds passed before they spoke again, "Ummm, yeah, it looks like everything is good in here. And my refrigerator is definitely running."

Tiana wasted no time to cash in on her joke, "Well you better go catch it!"

Doubling over with laughter as if she had told the world's funniest joke, she dropped her phone on the floor before she could end the call.

"What a bitch!" the prankee responded before ending the call.

I'll admit, I laughed a little. Ok, ok it was hilarious. Maybe the wine had finally settled into my system or maybe I too had completely lost my mind, but something in me wanted to give it a try. I grabbed Tiana's phone and my fingers automatically began to dial a number. It was like they had a mind of their own.

"Ouch!" I shouted. The phone released a burst of static electricity at the same time I heard the line connect. I stuck my thumb in my mouth to ease the pain while I waited for a response.

Silence.

We waited a few moments, but all we could hear from the other line was breathing.

After a minute or so of patterned breathing Tiana's patience was up, "Hello!" she shouted into the phone.

"Hello?" a voice whispered back, "Can you really hear me?"

"Duh," Tiana replied flatly.

"Finally!" the shallow voice exalted barely above a whisper, "I don't know how much time I have to talk. Can you help me?"

Tiana looked in my direction and immediately began to laugh, "Hahaha, funny joke Amina. Who did you call?"

Normally I hate being labeled the fearful friend, but in this situation, I was paralyzed by fear. The desperation in the woman's voice on the other end of the phone let me know that they were actually in some sort of trouble and I was not prepared to be a hero tonight.

"Amina, is that you?" the voice called out, "Can you help me?"

I shot Tiana a look of pure hatred. Why did she have to say my name?

"I have no idea who this is," I mouthed to Tiana.

Tiana shrugged her shoulders nonchalantly and took her final gulp of wine, *"Well then let's find out!"* she mouthed back.

I know better, but I blame the liquid courage for my next move.

"Of course I can help you, what's your name?" I asked, hoping I didn't sound as scared as I felt.

Silence.

"Hello? I said I will help you, but you have to tell me your name." I restated.

An unfamiliar voice responded, "I can't tell you my name, Amina. But I'm glad to finally meet you." This voice was sinister; much deeper than the whispery voice Tiana and I had originally engaged.

"Who is this? What happened to the girl?" Tiana asked, slightly slurring her words.

"I can't tell you my name either, Tiana," the creepy voice responded again.

Tiana looked up at me with sober eyes, *"How do they know my name?"* she mouthed.

The booming voice laughed into the phone.

"He knows everything," the faint voice of the scared woman said.

Before we could ask any more questions, the phone beeped, indicating that the call was disconnected.

"Holy shit!" Tiana screamed, throwing her phone across the room, "Whose number did you call?"

"I don't know," I said, "I don't even remember pressing the send button before the phone started ringing."

I attempted to shake it off, but I couldn't get the sound of that voice laughing out of my head. I put on the bravest voice I could muster, "Thank God, we used that texting app or we'd be screwed. I would hate for those weirdos to call us back."

Tiana nodded in agreement, and we decided that another bottle of wine was the only way to end this night. We made our way to my bedroom with an unopened bottle of wine in tow. The phone call had us so shaken up that we finished the new bottle of wine in no time.

"No more prank calling for me!" Tiana slurred as she placed her empty wineglass on the nightstand.

"I couldn't agree more," I yawned as a vino-induced sleep threatened to end our girl's night early.

Bundling up in my queen-sized bed, we prepared to let our dreams party the night away. Tiana nudged me just as my eyelids began to shut, "Do you think that was real?"

I smiled lazily, "Of course not. Those two were probably just as bored as we were. Now go to sleep," I yawned again. "We have to be at Kendra's party early tomorrow."

As soon as the words left my mouth, I realized that I had almost forgotten all about Kendra's party tomorrow. Of course we were helping set up, so I grabbed my cell phone to set the alarm. There is nothing worse than being late to a Kendra Carter event. With the alarm set, I drifted peacefully into dreamland.

"What's your name?" the toothless girl questioned.

"Amina. You say it like Aaaah-meeeeee-naaaa!" I responded. "What's your name?"

"Tiana, but you can call me T. Like the letter." She smiled that toothless smile and I knew immediately that she was going to be my best friend.

I was never one of those girls that dreamt about becoming a princess or finding a knight in shining armor. No, my dreams were always about the past. A constant slideshow of "Amina's Greatest Hits" was how I spent every night.

At least this was a decent memory.

Tiana and I were fast friends at the age of 6. I was a very timid and fearful 6-year old, and she was hell on wheels, to say the least. T was always on the move, and I could barely keep up. I even remember her running away from home a few times when we were younger. She would always show back up as if nothing had happened, but it was like she was a different person after each disappearance. Despite her inconsistency, I loved her. If I'm really honest with myself, I knew nothing of the world until I met T.

I had grown up in the home of divorced parents. Because neither parent wanted to be the one responsible for hurting me, I was completely sheltered. Now, I'm not complaining about my upbringing. I was well taken care of, but my parents had made me so afraid of the world that I stayed inside for most of my childhood. If it weren't for books and my friends, I would know nothing of the real world.

On the other end of the divorce spectrum was my friend Kendra, whom I also met when I was six. We saw each other for the first time in one of those kids of divorced parents' therapy groups. Her parents spoiled her rotten to account for the terrible divorce proceedings she witnessed. I mean she had everything and anything she had ever wanted--except her parents back together. I sat beside her every day for a month, afraid to utter a word. I could tell by the way she dressed that she was too cool to talk to me. And then one day, she spoke. She only asked if she could borrow a pen, but the conversations flowed effortlessly after that. In the 6th year of my life, I met my soulmates. And I can honestly say they are the best friends a girl could ask for.

Though my friendships with both of them were completely different, our friendship as a group felt natural. When Kendra,

Tiana, and myself all ended up at the same high school, you would have thought we had known each other all our lives; best friends was an understatement.

As my thoughts on friendship became background noise, my 6-year-old self faded into the distance. I then found myself staring at my reflection in a public restroom mirror. I realized that my dream had catapulted me to my least favorite place--high school. High school was such a blur, the only good things I remembered occurred with the girls, but it seemed I could only ever reconnect to those days in my dreams.

"Why do you even talk to her? She's so creepy!" Kendra asked while applying a fresh coat of Ruby Woo lipstick.

Wait a minute; I know this dream! I had only ever dreamt about this restroom scene, and I had always wondered who the hell we were talking about. At least I knew what to say next, "Because she's my friend. End of discussion."

"Well she's a crappy friend," Tiana chimed in.

"Give it a rest! She's always had my back!" I said.

Silence.

My friends disappeared right before my eyes, and darkness surrounded me. My eyes had adjusted to the dark moments before I was forced to cover my ears.

"HEEEEEEEEEEEEEEEEEEEELP!!!!" I heard a faint voice scream in the distance. "Help me!"

The patterned breathing and the desperation sounded familiar. This was the same voice from the prank call earlier that night. And then I heard the deep, raspy laugh from the phone call echoing around me. The laughter was getting closer. So close and so loud, in fact, that my body shook from the vibrations.

And then I felt the weight of hands on my shoulders.

My mind shifted to fight or flight mode and I woke up. On instinct, my body shot up in the bed. I tried to control my breathing, but I could still feel the vibrations from the demonic laughter in the dream.

BUZZZZZZZ BUZZ BUZZ BUZZZZZZZ

I considered walking around to locate the source of the buzzing, but I was still trying to catch my breath from the nightmare. A hollow silence had begun to creep into the room when a small, blinking light caught my eye. The silence didn't last because my phone began to vibrate again. I was receiving a text.

BUZZZZZZ BUZZ BUZZ BUZZZZZZ

I grabbed the phone from my nightstand to remedy the annoying buzzing. Something told me to check the time on my phone. To my surprise it was almost time to wake up, "How could it be so 11:30 already?"

I would normally see the sun peeking through the blinds by now, but the only light that could be seen was illuminating from the screen of my cell phone. Maybe, my clock was wrong. I placed my phone back on the nightstand and immersed myself in the covers. If the time was correct, then I knew my alarm was 5 minutes away from shattering any chance I had at going back to sleep. I definitely needed a little more rest before I had to deal with Queen Kendra.

BUZZZZZZZ BUZZ BUZZ BUZZZZZZZ

Another text.

BUZZZZZZZ BUZZ BUZZ BUZZZZZZZ

Another text.

"Who in the hell is texting me back to back like this?" I grumbled, hoping that it wasn't Jonathan. It had been a while since we had spoken, but our last interaction had not ended well.

I grabbed my phone again and saw that I had five text messages from the same sender. I didn't have the number saved in my phone. Maybe Jonathan got a new number? I nervously opened the texts, afraid of what he had to say this time. But it wasn't Jonathan.

+Unknown Sender

Can you help me Amina?

11:20am

+Unknown Sender

Can you help me Amina?

11:21am

+Unknown Sender

Can you HELP me Amina?

11:24am

+Unknown Sender

CAN YOU HELP ME AMINA!

11:29am

+Unknown Sender

AMINA!

11:32am

31

I didn't know who was texting me. I turned my phone off, but I can still hear the vibrations. I checked to see if my phone was actually off and it was.

I'm not sure if my mind is playing tricks on me or if Tiana's phone is to blame, but I can *still* hear the vibrations. And they are getting closer.

BUZZZZZZZ BUZZ BUZZ BUZZZZZZZ

"I found you!" a voice whispers directly in my ear.

I tried to fight whoever it was, but I couldn't move. I wanted to yell, but no sound came out. I felt hands on the side of my face. And the more I fought it, the sleepier I became.

I'm so sleepy.

I keep trying to open my eyes, but they are so heavy. I know that I can't hold them open any longer.

A burst of light took over the room…and then I saw her.

I remembered her.

CHAPTER 3: MY BEAUTIFUL NIGHTMARE

The Sandman must have run out of good dreams tonight. When my eyes shut, against my will, for the second time tonight, I drifted into another nightmare. Tonight, I was reminded of the day I met *him*.

I was rushing to my next class in my Junior year of high school when some jerk bumped into me and knocked all of my books on the floor. The perpetrator never even looked back to see what he had done. I knelt to the ground to pick up my belongings when Jonathan Richards sauntered over to help. Standing up, I smoothed out my teal sweater and allowed him to gather my things. I had heard through the grapevine that he was asking around about me, but he wasn't really my type. He was a major flirt and from what I had heard he had dated almost every girl in the school. After picking up my books, he flashed the whitest smile I had ever seen and offered to walk me to my locker.

I didn't say a word to him until we made it to my locker. Something about him made me so nervous that I could barely even speak. I couldn't even look at him because every time he looked at me I messed up my combination. After one too many minutes of total concentration, I successfully entered the combination into my locker.

"Thanks for your help," I said.

"No problem," he replied.

I swung the maroon door open and he placed my books in one by one. I hoped he hadn't noticed that I was staring at him the entire time.

He placed the last book in my locker and extended his hand in my direction, "I'm Jonathan." Another toothy smile.

I shook his hand but pulled back quickly. His skin was as soft as it looked and the way he shook my hand caused my temperature to rise. I hid my hands in the pockets of my dark denim jeans to hide my sweaty palms.

"Well, are you going to tell me your name?" he asked.

"Oh y-yeah," I stammered, "my name is Amina." I stuck my hand out again, like an idiot.

"Uh, we just did that," he laughed.

Real smooth, Amina.

"Just testing you," I retorted.

It was the best I could come up with on short notice. I was ready to flee the scene for fear of embarrassing myself further, but Jonathan seemed content with watching me squirm.

"Speaking of a test, you have Ms. Marshall's class next, right?" he pointed to the World History book I was still holding.

I nodded.

"How about we walk together?" he proposed.

Walking hand in hand to our World History class, I forgot all about my sweaty palms and all the rumors I had heard about him. For that moment, I was the happiest girl at Chamberlain High. But that moment was short-lived.

We dated for the rest of high school, and we even tried to do the long-distance thing when he went out of state for college. After Freshman year, I thought that we would be able to endure the time apart, but the distance proved to be too much in our Sophomore year. I was afraid of flying, and he was afraid of commitment, so we called it quits. I was content with just being friends, but he didn't take the breakup well. A chill came over my body as the dream drifted to the last time Jonathan and I had spoken.

This was the fifth time this week I had seen him sitting outside of my apartment. He parked a short distance away from the entrance, but I knew his car. He had been driving the same black, beat up Honda Civic since we were teenagers. I had learned to ignore his presence over the years, but seeing him parked in the shadows let me know that things were escalating. Instinct told me that the sudden decrease in voicemails and text messages was not a sign of maturity, but a girl could dream. Deep down, I knew he was harmless, but his inability to disconnect was unsettling. Just to be safe, I made sure to lock my doors and windows tonight.

I was sitting on the gray sectional he bought for me when I moved into this apartment at the end of Freshman year when curiosity got the best of me. Tiptoeing to the window that overlooked the street, I peeked through the flimsy blinds. I saw that his car was still there, but he was no longer sitting in the driver's seat. He was standing outside of the car, staring up at my window. I dropped to the floor, afraid that he had seen me.

I must have stayed crouched on the ground for five minutes before I had the courage to stand. Slowly, I stood back up and peeked through the blinds again. He was still there, and he was still staring. I felt the adrenaline rushing through my body and my skin began to tingle. The streetlight above Jonathan and his car began to flicker. He looked up at the light for a second and then immediately turned his gaze in my direction. The look on his face let me know that he could see me and when his mouth turned up into a grin, it felt like my heart was going to beat out of my chest. Simultaneously, the streetlight began to pulse with the pace of my heart. The more the light pulsed, the bigger Jonathan's smile became. I shut my eyes to hold back the tears, and I heard the light bulb shatter onto the sidewalk.

I opened my eyes and saw the shards of glass lining the cement...but I did not see Jonathan.

I backed away from the window and stumbled over what I believed to be the sectional. Attempting to regain my balance, I tried to grab the arm of the couch, but instead, I felt a hand. I turned to find Jonathan standing in my apartment with the same grin plastered on his face.

"What are you up here doing?" he asked, inching towards me.

"How did you get in here?" I shouted, backing up towards the kitchen. I needed to be near sharp objects in case he turned out to be not so harmless.

He jingled a key ring in my face, "The landlord remembered me from when I lugged this sectional up those stairs." He patted the sectional with his free hand and let his fingers caress the microfiber as he continued his pursuit.

"I answered your question, now answer mine." he commanded, stopping short of the kitchen.

"I don't know what you're talking about Jonathan, but you need to get out of here!" I yelled. I reached for my cell phone, "Don't make me call the police."

He threw his head back and released a guttural laugh, "I'm not worried about that. All I want to know is what you are doing up here. What did you do to the light?"

By this time, I had my hand in the drawer with all of the knives. If he continued this insane behavior I would be forced to protect myself, "Jonathan, listen, I don't know what happened to the light. I don't know why you are watching my apartment, but if you don't stop harassing me I will call the police!"

Without warning, he charged forward. I flung the drawer open in front of me, grabbing the biggest, sharpest knife I owned. Knife in hand, I took a step back.

"You better get out of here!" I said, slashing in his direction.

There was something about his eyes tonight that I had never seen before, something dark and unknown. Despite my warning, he did not back away. In fact, he came closer.

"I found you again!" he shouted, but the voice coming out of Jonathan's mouth was not his own.

I darted past him back into the living room, but he followed. This time he got the best of me. He pushed me against the wall closest to the door and pinned my hands above my head. I was still holding the knife, but he had such a tight grip on my wrists that I could not use it.

"Mine, mine, mine!" the voice coming from Jonathan's mouth repeated. He was now sniffing my hair as I felt his free hand grab for my knife.

Just as he was peeling my last finger from the blade, the living room door flung open.

An animal had burst its way inside my apartment and pinned Jonathan to the ground, at least I thought it was an animal. Elongated brown strands of hair covered its entire body, it had a snout, and it stood atop hooves. I would have been 100% sure it was an animal until it turned to me and yelled...

"RUN!" the beast shouted.

My mind wanted to run, but my legs wouldn't move.

"J-J-Jonathan what's happening?" I questioned.

The beast turned to face me again, "This is NOT Jonathan. Don't stop running until you feel safe." The beast was struggling to hold Jonathan down, "Get out of here, you need to RUN!" the word run came out as more of a growl.

That was enough to kick start the engine in my legs. I ran out of my apartment and down the street as fast as I could, never looking back.

I could still taste remnants of the power that shot through my system on the day I escaped the Wall. Imagine my surprise when I discovered that power this great was being harbored in a female human. I scoured this dimension for years to find her. I looked in parallel universes and many different time periods to satiate this hunger, but nothing and no one compared to her.

To the Realms, I am known as The Memory Thief. Had I been given a say, I would much prefer to be called the Night Prince. I hate the word thief. Besides, memories are meant to be shared so why should my hobby be labeled a crime?

"Because they need to villainize you."

I could feel the girl they called Amina tossing and turning in her sleep. I had visited her in the dream, but a Guardian was there waiting for me. The Guardian helped the girl escape. The woman in white must have told them about me when she stopped

me from taking the girl's powers earlier this evening.

"She will never let you reach the power."

I ignored the hissing. I hated it when they talked over my

thoughts.

I never expected to see the woman in white again after *she*

left me in the darkness. Behind the Wall, I imagined that *she* was

just another voice in my head, but seeing *her* again let me know

that *she* was real.

"Kill the woman in white!"

Again, I ignored the pestering voices shouting in unison. I

peered into the sleeping girl's mind for just a moment longer. The

girl's heroine may have stopped me from taking her powers, but

she could not keep me from the girl's dreams. One touch was all I

needed to mark her. Unfortunately, a touch was not enough to

grant me her power. No, I would need to do much more for that.

"Kill the girl! Kill the girl! Kill the girl!"

Caving in, I responded to the voices within, "Killing the girl will not be easy; she is well protected," I paced back and forth, piecing together a plan.

"Killing the girl will be very easy. It's always easy!"

The looping vision of myself ripping through Amina's flesh was pushed into my mind. The thought alone brought me immense pleasure, but I know that subtlety would work best in this situation.

Digging through her memories left much to be desired. The Guardians had locked down her mind before I could readily explore. They had only left me with one useful memory to work with. The memory was ten years old and a bit distorted, but I was able to determine a location for the one called Amina. I breathed in the smell of fresh grass clippings as I trudged through the deep red clay to my destination. Standing at the base of the steps of Chamberlain High School in Atlanta, GA, I could no longer contain my excitement.

I stopped to admire a rose bush at the entrance of the school. I have always loved roses; they were the only flowers that would bloom in the darkness behind the Wall. I picked a flower from the bush and proceeded to walk up the steps. I plucked a petal with each ascending stair "She loves me; she loves me not. She loves me...she loves me not...She loves me...she loves me not!" I yelled as the last petal hit the ground.

"No one will ever love you like we do!"

"Here he goes again, always playing with the flowers."

"Do you remember the plan?"

"Of course I remember the plan," I snapped, "It's my plan!"

I was sick of their condescending comments. I swung the door open to the school, but before I walked in I placed the now empty stem of the rose in my mouth and swallowed it whole. I could feel the thorns scraping their way down, and I laughed when the voices began to scream out in pain.

"Now kindly, shut up," I commanded, "I have work to do."

CHAPTER 4: THE AWAKENING

I awoke from a dream that I could not easily decipher. One minute I was dreaming about Jonathan, and then things got really weird --Jonathan has never tried to hurt me, well, at least not physically. And then that monster just came out of nowhere. The sound of his growl is still ringing in my ears. I'm so used to my dreams being actual memories that last night's dream going off book has me really shaken up.

"Amina, honey, are you ready?" my mother shouted, interrupting my thoughts.

Rather than answer, I simply head towards the stairs. I reached for the doorknob and quickly pulled my hand back from the shock. As I was walking down the hall, I got the feeling that last night's weirdness had seeped into the morning. I can't remember the last time I had visited my mother, but here I am.

On top of that, I had a pounding headache, and I felt really off. Maybe a little breakfast is all I need? As I made my way to the kitchen, I tripped. "When did we put a table here?" I mumbled to myself, rubbing my knee. I looked up and was even more surprised to see a bedazzled mirror above this imposter table. I haven't seen this mirror since—

The mirror's reflection startled me.

I didn't have a chance to register what I had just seen. I heard footsteps and then the sound of my mother's voice, "Mina, are you ready for school?"

I turned around and I couldn't hide my reaction.

"What's wrong Amina? You look like you've seen a ghost," she said.

I continued to stare at the woman who was now awaiting my response. She stood there in a gray and black dress suit with her hands on her hips. She was definitely my mother, but a much younger version of the mother I had just video chatted with the day before.

My eyes wandered back to the mirror beside me, and I was reminded of my distorted reflection in the mirror. If I thought my mom looked young, I looked even younger. I lightly touched the deep brown hair that was neatly placed in a thick, coarse bun on top of my head. I allowed my fingers to caress the sepia skin that was as smooth as marble on my face. My mouth hung open as I continued to explore the reflection looking back at me and I caught a glimpse of my teeth; they were perfectly straight. I ran my tongue over my teeth and I felt something shift onto my gums. Opening my mouth again for a closer look, I noticed the invisible retainer. I hadn't worn a retainer since I was--

"Are you deaf or something Amina? How many times do I have to ask if you are ready to go?" my mother asked again.

I nodded a yes to keep from opening my mouth for fear that I would vomit all over her nice dress.

"How are you ready if you are still in pajamas?" she glanced at her watch, "If we don't leave this house in 30 minutes, you will have to take the bus. Go to your room and get dressed!" she commanded, pointing back up the stairs.

I didn't want to upset her any further so I quickly made my way back to my bedroom. I closed the door and began to inspect my surroundings. Everything around me looked like it has gone through a time warp. My walls are covered with posters of has-been teenage musicians and everything, I mean everything, is covered in glitter. I plopped onto my bed and scratched my head. The retainer, the Hello Kitty pajamas, the nagging mom...these three things had not all been under the same roof since I was 16 years old.

Wait! My mom keeps shouting about getting ready for school. Is she talking about high school? I must still be asleep. This has never happened before. I'm used to having lucid dreams, but this dream feels a little too real.

Lifting my legs under the cover, I laid back in the full size, puffy, pink bed and closed my eyes. I know that the only way to wake up from this dream is to sleep. I waited patiently for reality to pull me back. When I felt the covers being ripped off of me, I just knew that I was back in my apartment with Tiana.

I was wrong.

"Amina, are you kidding me? That's it! You're riding the bus!" the younger version of my mother shouted before leaving and slamming the bedroom door behind her.

I couldn't move.

I looked out the window hoping for some sort of explanation to why I was still dreaming. After staring at the leaves fall from the trees for entirely too long, I decided to get dressed and go through the motions. Hopefully, it would push me through

REM sleep to the other side. I rummaged through my teeny bopper closet, searching for something that wasn't awful. My hands lingered on a teal sweater. The cashmere sweater was so soft that I couldn't help myself. Rubbing the soft material against my skin, I hoped this sweater would provide the comfort I needed to get me through what promised to be a very long day. I threw on a pair of denim jeans and grabbed a pair of black boots. These were always my favorite Fall boots when I was younger. As I buckled the strap on the boot, I considered something I had never considered before. I began to wonder if this could be real. I pinched myself so many times that my arm started to bruise, but I just can't bring myself to believe that this is my reality. Who am I kidding? I know for a fact that this is a dream. I guess I'm in a really deep sleep. The way my body felt, I must have had a really rough day yesterday. I'll just let this dream play itself out until I wake up, which I hope is sooner rather than later.

After eating breakfast, I caught the city bus to school. Remembering the route was easy. I often took the bus when I was younger. According to my mom, I was always moving too slow for a ride. When the bus pulled up to Chamberlain High, I looked around to gauge the level of uncertainty and disbelief on the other passenger's faces. But to my surprise, no one else even noticed that I didn't belong. I was alone in my confusion.

A woman brushes past me as I slowly descend the stairs to exit the bus. Despite my internal reaction to her rudeness, I have made the choice to smile and be as pleasant as possible on the outside. Besides, I know no matter how I feel, I can't change anything in this dream. I smile a little at the thought of pushing her back, but quickly banish the madness to the back of my mind. Forgetting is my best option in this case.

Walking towards the entrance of the school, it dawns on me that I don't remember ever dreaming of this day before. Most of high school was a blur to me. I rarely dreamed of the time I spent there, but it was also rare that I had new dreams. At least today would be interesting.

Staring up the steps at the building where I had spent four years of my life, I had no idea what I was about to see. I just hoped

I was ready. "Just focus on being 16. Blend into the crowd," I mumbled, giving myself a pep talk before I made my way inside.

"What are you talking about?" A voice quizzed.

I recognized that voice. I turned around to see a familiar face staring back at me with a raised eyebrow. It was Tiana, well 16-year-old Tiana.

"What are *you* talking about?" I threw back at her, hoping she hadn't heard what I'd said.

She rolled her eyes, "Amina, I'm not in the mood to go around in circles with you today. I had the worst night ever!"

Tiana began to ramble on about her night, but I was lost in my thoughts. As usual, Tiana was focused on herself. Her narcissism worked in my favor as I'm sure she did not hear what I had said, either that or she didn't care. I looked back at my best friend who was still talking about the night before and for the first time in a long time, I was taken aback by her beauty. Her ruddy-brown hair was styled into a beautiful pixie cut and framed her face perfectly. Her sun-kissed tawny skin was the perfect backdrop for her deep hazel angular eyes. Those eyes that always caused the boys to guess that she was born on some exotic island, but the funny thing is, she isn't mixed with anything –she is simply a beautiful, black girl. I laughed thinking of all of the places she would lie about being from.

"What's so funny?" she asked, finally acknowledging my presence.

"Nothing," I responded.

I noticed someone waving at me from a distance, but I couldn't make out who it was. I waved back, and the person began to approach.

"Oh, fuck!" Tiana said and pulled me into the school building. She dragged me into the restroom before I could see who was coming.

"What was that all about? Who was that?" I asked.

"She's so annoying!" Tiana stated, propping herself up on the restroom sink. I could tell that she hadn't heard my question.

Like clockwork, Kendra walked into the restroom and locked the door behind her.

"You saw her too?" Tiana sniggered.

"Yes," Kendra sighed.

"Saw who?" I asked, desperate to be in on this secret.

"Your little friend, Charity," Tiana answered. She mocked the waving person I had seen moments before.

"Why do you even talk to her? She's so creepy!" Kendra asked while applying a fresh coat of Ruby Woo lipstick.

Wait a minute; I know this dream! I had only ever dreamt about this restroom scene, and I had always wondered who the hell we were talking about. At least I knew what to say next, "Because she's my friend. End of discussion."

"Well she's a crappy friend," Tiana chimed in.

"Give it a rest! She's always had my back!" I said.

I gave myself a round of applause in my head. I would strongly consider taking up acting when I finally woke up. The room fell silent and I waited patiently to see what unfolded next.

Tap. Tap. Tap.

"It's her!" Kendra whispered, "Don't open the door!" she said staring directly at me.

Tap. Tap. Tap.

I walked towards the door. I really wanted to open the door to see who was on the other side. I knew if it wasn't supposed to happen, the dream wouldn't let me open it, but I walked towards the door anyway just to build up the drama. Maybe it would even wake me up. Plus, it's my dream I should be allowed to have a little fun. To my surprise, I walked over to the door and unlocked it with ease. I guess this is how it happened originally. I wonder why I never saw this part when I dreamt about this before. The door opened and my jaw dropped.

"Hey Amina," the frail girl with the acne covered, mocha skin smiled. Her lip got caught on her braces, but she didn't seem to care. I took a closer look at her clothes and it clicked that this was the "she" that had waved at me outside and this was also the girl that Kendra and Tiana were just griping about.

"Hi." I uttered, afraid to look away.

"Seriously, Amina?" Kendra fumed, "I'm out of here." She stormed out of the restroom, with a disgusted look on her face.

"Me too." Tiana scoffed, pushing through the girl and myself while exiting the restroom.

I stared in disbelief as the girl shuffled into the restroom and made her way to the sink.

"They suck. I will never understand how you all are so close. You are way too good for them." she stated.

"I know right." was all I could muster.

"Is everything okay?" she asked, pushing her frazzled hair away from her face.

I took a deep breath, "Of course," I lied.

"Okay, well I'll talk to you later. Oh, and be careful with those two," she said as she scurried out of the restroom.

The door closed behind her and I dropped my things on the floor and grabbed onto the sink. Jesus, I could barely catch my breath. I couldn't come to terms with what I had just seen. My mother's words echoed in my head. *What's wrong Amina? You look like you've seen a ghost.* This time I really had seen a ghost. I haven't seen Charity in years! For some reason I couldn't quite remember what happened, but I remember hearing that she had died. We were so close when we were younger, but I don't remember us speaking much after this year.

I pried myself from the sink, long enough to lock the door. Pacing back and forth while talking to myself I tried to figure all of this out. I couldn't understand why I was dreaming about this memory. What was so special about today? And why could my mind remember this day, second by second, but it couldn't remember what happened to Charity? I tried to think back, but my mind felt sluggish. I walked back to the sink to splash cold water on my face, hoping it would wake me up.

"What kind of dream is this? I am never able to do whatever I want in these dreams, but now I can. What is going on? I need to wake up! This is so craz--" My rant was interrupted.

BUZZZZZZZ BUZZ BUZZ BUZZZZZZZ

I froze when I heard the buzzing. I remembered that sound from my nightmares. The lights in the restroom flickered, and I darted towards a stall.

BUZZZZZZZ BUZZ BUZZ BUZZZZZZZ

I closed my eyes when the restroom fell under total darkness. The room was pitch black, except for a blinking light in my purse. I rolled my eyes and stuck my hand in the bag. *Not again.* I felt the vibrations getting stronger. My suspicion was correct. I lifted the phone from the purse and the lights came back on in the restroom. It was just a text.

+2046598265

Will you help me Amina?

8:50am

CHAPTER 5: THE GIRL THAT NO ONE KNEW

"What's' your name again?" the scraggly girl questioned, stuffing one of the complimentary powdered donuts into her mouth.

I leaned back in the uncomfortable chair and watched the stragglers fill in the circle. This was the first meeting I had attended without Kendra.

"My name is Amina," I responded. All I could think was that without Kendra by my side, I had no reason to talk to anyone else.

The girl stuck her hand out, "I'm Charity."

I unwillingly shook her hand, "Nice to meet you."

I stared down at my notebook, hoping she would take the hint. She didn't.

"It's my first time here," she shared, "have you come before?"

I couldn't help but remember my first meeting and how lonely I felt with no one to talk to, so I engaged.

"Yeah, I've been coming for a while. My parents have been divorced for," I counted on my fingers, "three whole years now."

Charity's voice clouded over, "My parents just got divorced about a month ago."

I placed my hand on hers, "It's not your fault."

She gripped my hand a little tighter, "Thanks."

Charity had spent her entire life hoping to remain unseen. Being the daughter of an overworked, single mother and a deadbeat didn't come with many perks. The stress hadn't been good for her; she had a face full of acne and no friends to show for it. All of her clothing was either from Goodwill or a hand-me-down that was two years out of season. But as the saying goes, beggars can't be choosers. By ten years old, she had her entire life mapped out in her head:

The day that Charity met Amina Wallace had started like any ordinary day, but she could have never prepared for how it would end. Charity's parents had just split up and the state was paying for her to attend a therapy group for the kids of divorce. She could sense that Amina wasn't very outgoing, but she decided to talk to her anyway. After they had broken the ice, Charity was convinced that Amina was the nicest person she had met in her entire life. Imagine her surprise when she went from no friends to two friends in that same day.

While walking home from the therapy session, Charity bumped into a man passing out candy in front of a new grocery store; Guardian's Groceries. His face was painted chalk white and a bright red smile had been drawn on. The red and yellow pinstriped pants he wore were accentuated by an oversized bright orange vest with red and yellow polka dots. Normally, Charity was afraid of clowns, but something about this clown's emotionless eyes intrigued her. She didn't want to admit it, but he reminded her of her father.

"Sorry, I'm such a spaz," she apologized to the performer.

The man didn't utter a word, but he did offer her a candy bar. She took the candy with no hesitation. It had been ages since she had tasted name brand chocolate. She scarfed the candy bar down in three large bites.

"Slow down little lady, there's more," said the clown.

Licking the last bit of chocolate off of her finger she asked, "Where?"

The man with the empty eyes stepped aside and gestured towards the storefront, "Everything you'll need is inside."

She looked to the clown and then looked to the door which led down a dark corridor in the building. Logic didn't have a chance to set in because her stomach growled and all she could think was that she really wanted another candy bar.

"Thanks mister," she said walking into the store.

"The pleasure is all mine," he responded.

There weren't any lights on in the inside of the building, but her feet seemed to know where to go. Halfway down the corridor, Charity stopped and turned around to see if the clown man was still on the street offering candy to passersby, but he was gone. Continuing on her path, she hit a dead end. She ran her hands across the grainy cement that stood between her and the outside world and came to the conclusion that she had missed a turn somewhere in the darkness. She turned around and ran back towards the door that led to the street, hoping to get some guidance from the clown. She was happy to see that her clown friend had returned. But that happiness didn't last for long. She realized that he was closing the door.

"Wait, don't close the door!" she yelled, waving her hands in the air to grab his attention.

He looked up at Charity, and they locked eyes for a brief moment, but he did not yield. She was less than a foot away from the exit when he closed the glass door in her face and locked it from the outside.

"Please let me out!" she begged.

For the first time since she had bumped into him on the street, his mouth spread into a smile, "I can't let you out. We need you."

"We?" she asked looking around, "No one is here but you and me."

He pointed back down the corridor, "Go back to the other end. They are waiting for you."

"No way, mister. Let me out!!" she shouted, banging on the glass door. With every strike, she had hoped that the door would shatter, but the door didn't even tremble.

Still pointing towards the end of the dark corridor he emphasized, "Everything you need is down there."

Charity stood banging at that door for 5 minutes, but in those 5 minutes, the clown never moved a muscle. He continued to point and she continued to bang on the door. By the time she stopped, the back of her shirt was covered in sweat and she was struggling to catch her breath. Once she realized that his instruction was more of a command, she began her walk back down the corridor.

Her mind raced with each step. She thought of how stupid she had been to end up in this situation. Not only did she know better than to talk to strangers, but to be lured into a building by candy from a stranger had to be an all-time record for stupid.

Unlike before when she reached the end of the corridor, this time she was face to face with a door. Instinct told her to look back to see if the clown man was still watching, but just like before he had vanished. A loud creaking sound was released, when she opened the door. From where she was standing, she could tell that the room on the other side of the door offered significantly more breathing room than the corridor, so she walked in. The room was dark, but as soon as she stepped across the threshold the fluorescent lights on the ceiling came on. Like a domino effect, the lights came on one by one until the interior of the room was visible.

"Welcome Charity, we've been waiting for you," someone said.

The last light had just turned on. Like a spotlight, this light revealed a girl who appeared to be Charity's age sitting in a chair at the far end of the room. The room was all white; white ceiling tiles, white paint on the walls, and white laminate on the floors; and empty, except for two chairs.

"Who are you?" Charity asked. She hadn't moved since the lights began to come on, so she was still standing near the door.

The girl stood to her feet and presented a warm smile, "I'm a friend. Come," she motioned for Charity to take the seat beside her.

Shaking her head, no, Charity began to back up towards the door. She held her hand behind her back and was reaching for the knob when she heard it slam shut.

"I thought you wanted some more candy," the girl stated. She pulled three candy bars out of her purse and held them in Charity's direction.

Involuntarily, Charity licked her lips and the memories of how good the first candy bar had tasted flooded her mind. She thought back to the two locked doors that now stood between her and the building's exit and chose the lesser of two evils. Looking the girl over, Charity came to the conclusion that if push came to shove she could take her.

The girl spoke again, "Come on Charity, which one of these is your favorite? I've got a Snickers bar, a Butterfinger, and a Baby Ruth."

Weighing her options one more time, Charity decided to sit with the girl. Strangely, the closer Charity got to the girl, the more comfortable she felt. By the time Charity was standing in front of her designated chair, she didn't feel intimidated at all.

"Sit with me, Charity," the girl suggested, patting the seat beside hers.

Charity complied with the request, but her eyes never left the three candy bars in the girl's hand.

"Can I have them?" she asked, pointing to the candy.

The girl laughed, "Of course you can, but I need a favor from you first," She looked around the room as if someone else was there besides the two of them, "I need you to keep a secret."

"I can do that. I promise I don't have anyone to tell." Charity responded, only half-jokingly.

Cocking her head to the side, the girl probed, "You sure about that, Charity? Not even your new friend, Amina?"

Hearing Amina's name caused Charity to jump out of her chair. Having just met Amina hours before, she could not understand how this strange girl could know that.

"Who are you?" Charity asked again standing behind her chair. She knew that running was not a good option, but if she didn't like the girl's answer she needed to be ready to make a move.

"I told you I'm a friend, but you can call me Zion if you'd like." The girl patted the seat beside her once more, "Sit back down, Charity. I'll tell you whatever you want to know."

The girls stared at each other for a few seconds before something motivated Charity to move. She hesitated before taking the seat next to Zion, but something inside of her trusted the little girl. Zion handed Charity the Snickers bar.

Candy in one cheek, Charity began probing Zion for answers again, "How do you know me? I never told you my name, but you knew it."

Avoiding the question, Zion revisited her earlier request, "I will give you these other two candy bars if you promise to keep my secret, Charity."

Charity swallowed her last bite of the Snicker bar, "Ok, I promise."

Zion handed over the two remaining candy bars, "Let's shake on it to make it official."

Charity extended her chocolate stained hand and Zion accepted.

When they released each other's hands, Charity rattled off a list of questions, "You got your promise, Zion, now answer my questions. How did you know my name? And what was with the question about Amina? How do *you* even know Amina?"

Zion leaned back in her chair before speaking, "You know, we have a lot in common, Charity. Much like myself, you are a girl that prefers not to be the center of attention. That is a very rare quality to find in people these days." She paused for a moment, unsure if she was ready to reveal her secret. She took a deep breath and continued, "I know who you are because it is my responsibility to know everyone in Amina Wallace's life. But I knew from the moment I saw you that you were the one we've been searching for."

Charity had already unwrapped the Butterfinger and taken a few bites as Zion spoke. She swallowed hard at Zion's last words, "Searching for me for what, exactly?"

Zion looked around the empty room again before answering, "You are the one we need to protect Amina from her enemies."

Charity laughed so hard that she almost spit out her Butterfinger.

Zion continued, "It sounds crazy. I know it does, but it's true. Amina is a very special girl. She is an integral piece in a long-awaited prophecy and there are some very bad people that don't want to see that prophecy fulfilled."

Charity lost her appetite. Placing the Baby Ruth in her back pocket for later, she spoke freely, "And what are we supposed to do about that?" Charity gave Zion a once over, "What are you, maybe ten years old like me? How do we stop bad guys from hurting another ten-year-old? We're not the Power Rangers." She laughed at her own joke, but Zion was not amused.

Zion stood from her chair and hovered over Charity. She began to crack her neck, and Charity could see that her face was beginning to shift. The sweet-faced, little girl that had coaxed her into the room seemed to be fading away and someone entirely different emerged. The thick curly afro that once covered the top of her head elongated and straightened out. Her skin began to darken and she lifted her eyes to mine. Never breaking eye contact with Charity, Zion smiled revealing a mouth full of braces.

Charity gasped, it was as if she was looking into a mirror.

Zion tossed her head from side to side, and the mask of the fair skinned girl with the curly afro and straight pearly white teeth was back in place, "I am not ten years old. This girl you see sitting here before you is for your benefit. I have been alive for centuries, Charity, but I have never had a more important task. My job is to protect this dimension, and that begins and ends with protecting Amina Wallace."

Charity finally broke her silence, "Why Amina? What does the prophecy say about Amina?"

Zion sat beside Charity and grabbed her hand, "I'll show you."

Charity saw the transition of the Earth through Zion's eyes. Everything was as expected until flames engulfed the planet.

"What's happening?" Charity whispered.

"The place you see is not your home, but it could have been. Many centuries ago, the Earth was ripped apart by quarreling nations. The planet imploded upon itself after becoming a nuclear wasteland. The place you live now, though known to you as the Planet Earth is actually the Second Earth."

The scene sped up until Zion and Charity stood in an empty wasteland.

"Where are we?" Charity asked.

Zion stared woefully into the distance, "This is what Second Earth was destined to become before the Innocents arrived. The prophecy I spoke of earlier promised prosperity to another dimension, but when the Innocents were brought here for safekeeping the prophecy adapted."

Zion waved her outstretched hand across the horizon and the scenery changed. There were people everywhere. The aroma of fresh bread lingered in the air and Charity recognized the sounds of the city, but she was still confused.

"Now, where are we?"

Zion explained, "This is Second Earth's current path. The arrival of the Innocents skewed the fate of the planet to that of peace and prosperity, but only as long as the Innocents are alive. So as you can see, it is critical that we keep Amina safe."

Charity nodded in agreement, but she still had questions, "And what about the bad people? Why would anyone want to stop this from happening?"

The scene faded to black.

Zion turned to face Charity, "Because we made a choice to save our realm at the cost of another," a tear rolled down her cheek and she quickly wiped it away with her free hand, "I mentioned that the prophecy of prosperity was originally intended for a different realm. The unfulfilled prophecy caused that realm to sink into anarchy. When the survivors of the destruction realized what had happened, they made it very clear that if they could not have the Innocents no one could. We were protected for many years, but as the old saying goes, nothing lasts forever."

Zion released Charity's hand and they were back in the all-white room. They stood in silence, gathering themselves from the journey.

Eventually, Zion cleared her throat, "So what do you think? Will you help us?"

"I don't know why you chose me, but I'm in." Charity stated, "what do I need to do?"

From that day forward, Zion and Charity were inseparable.

Zion explained to Charity that her role in the big picture would be that of Amina's cloak. That meant that if anyone ever came looking for Amina, they would find Charity first. It would then be Charity's responsibility to notify the Guardians that Amina was in danger.

It seemed simple enough.

To prepare for the inevitable, Charity was required me to meet up with Zion once a week for training. Until now, Charity had always resented her mother's work schedule. But with her mother always away at her first or second job, she never had to explain where she disappeared to in the middle of the week or where all of the bruises came from.

"Do we have to do this every week?" Charity asked, rolling up her sleeve to expose the vein.

Zion continued to prep, "The infusions are critical. It's more important than anything that you have a sufficient ratio of Amina's markers in your blood," She stopped prepping and looked into Charity's eyes, "The types of creatures that are looking for Amina do not have a copy of her school photo. The things that go bump in the night are almost always searching for blood. If your blood says that you are Amina, then they will believe it."

The routine was always the same. After the blood infusions, Zion would quiz Charity on Amina. If Charity was unable to answer the questions as if she was Amina, then she would be punished. The punishments would range from sensory deprivation to full out hostage torture. Zion believed it was important that Charity could tolerate all aspects of torture without cracking under pressure and revealing her true identity. Over time, Charity proved herself to be exactly who they needed. She always learned from her mistakes and soon enough the punishments became a distant memory. The more time Zion and Charity spent together the closer they became.

Four years went by and though Charity enjoyed her friendship with Amina, it was strictly business, but it was obvious that she and Zion had become best friends. The two spent as much time as they could together, but one day that all stopped.

It had been a few days since Charity had last heard from Zion. It wasn't unusual for Zion to go silent from time to time, but she always texted Charity on the burner phone when they had training. And today was a training day. Rather than be late and suffer through an earned punishment, Charity showed up at Guardian's Groceries at their usual time. She tried the front door but it was locked, which had never happened before, at least not to keep Charity out. She walked around to the back door and was able to get in. As she approached the training room, she could hear hushed voices on the other side of the door.

"Zion going missing is not a good sign," a male voice stated.

"I agree, but we don't need to panic. Zion disappears from time to time. I'm sure she'll be back tomorrow." another male voice responded.

"Yeah, she disappears from time to time but never on a training day." A third voice inserted.

Charity wondered if these were the people Zion was always looking around for. She wanted to peek into the room to see who was talking, but she knew better. That door was loud and creaky, and these could very realistically be "the bad guys".

"And what about the cloak?" the original voice questioned.

"Let's activate her, just in case." the second voice suggested.

Charity's heart began to pound. She ran out of the back door of the building as fast as she could. Her mind was racing: *Activate me! I knew exactly what that meant. Number one, these were not the bad guys, but things were indeed bad. If I needed to be activated, then this was not a test or a drill; something or*

someone had gotten through the Wall.

CHAPTER 6: THE FALLEN

From the moment I heard that I was activated, I was on high alert. Being Amina's cloak had taken a turn for the worst. Although I still hadn't heard from Zion, I knew that I needed to keep up appearances with Amina. I reached for my cell phone in the drawer of my nightstand and my hand brushed by the burner cell that Zion had given me. I didn't want to think about Zion today, so I grabbed my cell phone and closed the drawer:

Me

Hey Amina, are we

still on for the mall?

4:45pm

Amina

Of course! Meet you at 5:30!

4:46pm

Amina and I always hung out at the mall on Tuesdays. Her other friends had other obligations on Tuesdays, so it allowed Amina and me to be alone. When I arrived at the mall, I saw that Amina's bike was already locked onto the bike rack. If she beat me here, then I already knew where she was. After locking my bike up, I made my way to the bookstore near the Food Court. As suspected, I found her wandering up and down the Self-Help aisles.

"What problem are you trying to solve today Amina?" I asked. She jumped at the sound of my voice.

"You scared me," she whispered. Running her hands along the spines of the books on the shelf in front of her she filled me in, "I'm trying to learn more about the weird dreams I'm always having."

Amina was always going on and on about her dreams and how they always felt so real. Zion had never told me what Amina's powers were, but if I had to guess it would definitely have something to do with her weird dreams. I had sworn never to tell Amina that she was special. In fact, I often tried to downplay the bizarre stories she would tell me to keep her grounded.

I took a seat at the table between the bookshelves, "Have you found anything interesting?"

Amina pointed at the table I was currently sitting at, "Yep. Wanna help me read through those?"

I took inventory of the pile of books Amina was referring to. There were at least six books on the table, and each book had to be at least 300 pages. I organized the pile until one of the titles caught my eye, *The Age of the Innocents.*

"Amina, where did you get this one?" I asked, holding the book up in the air.

She turned to face me and squinted a little. She walked back to the table and grabbed the book from my hands.

"I didn't pick this up. This doesn't even say anything about dreams," she tossed the book back on the table, "someone else must have left it behind." She walked back over to the bookshelves and continued her search.

Grabbing the book, I flipped through the first few pages. I didn't have to read far to determine that this book had not been accidentally left behind. Someone had placed it here for Amina to find. I stood up from the table and began to look around, afraid of what I may find. I walked a few aisles over and shoved the book in between a southern cookbook and a book about potions. Whoever left this behind was going to have an adventure locating it. I hurried back to where Amina had been standing, but she was gone.

"Amina!" I shouted, "where did you go?"

I was terrified that I had lost her. Another friend, gone. I was running up and down the aisles when I bumped into someone head first.

"Why are you shouting?" Amina asked, rubbing her forehead, "I just went to get some water."

I thought of a lie, "I get nervous when I'm left alone in public places."

She grabbed my hand and helped me up, "I'm sorry, Charity, I'll keep that in mind. But let's go back to the table. I want to see if any of those books can tell me why my dreams feel so real."

I trailed behind Amina with my head on a swivel the entire time. We made it to the table without any strange occurrences, so I let my guard down.

"What happened to that book you showed me earlier?" Amina asked, pushing the books around on the table.

I shrugged, "I guess the person came back for it." Another lie.

"Oh well," she responded, "let's read!"

We spent the next two hours skimming the pages of the books Amina had selected. Amina didn't find what she was looking for, but she did come to a conclusion about the dreams she had been having. She shared her theory as we unlocked our bikes from the rack.

"You know one of those books talked about dream walking. It's this idea that a person can actually transport themselves to different times and places in their dreams. So, maybe I'm a time traveler," she giggled.

I smirked, "Well let's skip to the part where we are both rich and famous."

She closed her eyes and pretended to sleep. Opening her eyes, she shook her head from side to side, "It didn't work, but I'll try again tonight."

We laughed before going our separate ways. Her house was only a few minutes away, but I had a long ride ahead of me. The entire ride home all I could think of was that weird book. How did it end up on the table with Amina's stuff? I suppose that I should have been paying more attention to my surroundings because I looked up and had to swerve to miss a person standing on the sidewalk. My front tire hit a rock and sent me flying into the grass. When I regained my composure, the person I had swerved to miss was standing over me.

"Protect the girl!" they hissed. The person was wearing all black and their face was covered with a hood.

"What th--" I began.

"PROTECT THE GIRL!" the hooded person hissed again before running off into the woods behind me. The person, or whatever it was ran off on all fours like a cheetah.

I did not wait for them to return with any further instruction. Hopping on my bike, I rode home at the speed of light. I ran to my room and pulled open the drawer to my nightstand. I stared at the burner cell hoping to see a new message, but I knew better. I hadn't heard anything from Zion since I was 14 years old. Two years had flown by and no matter how hard I tried to keep up appearances, at this point, I was just another 16-year-old loser. The Charity that was going to save the world disappeared with Zion.

I woke up the next morning feeling drained. My dreams consisted of hooded shadows and Zion. I knew I needed to move on and let her go, but she had been my only real friend. I just couldn't bring myself to believe what had become so obvious at this point.

It was a school day, so I forced myself out of bed to get dressed. Most of my laundry was dirty, so I threw on what was available; a dark pink t-shirt from the thrift store, a light pink skirt my mom swore was vintage (which really just meant she got it from Goodwill), and my favorite gray hoodie. I hugged the hoodie tight to my chest. Zion had bought me this hoodie around this time of year, many years ago. The leaves had just started to change colors and we decided to go for a walk after training. My mind drifted to the past:

"Do you own any jackets that don't have holes in them?"
Zion questioned, sticking her finger into the hole that exposed my forearm.

I swatted her hand away, but she found another hole to invade.

"My mom just gets me what she can, when she can. You know that." I answered, now completely embarrassed.

We kept walking and stumbled upon a family-owned general store.

"Let's look around in here," Zion suggested.

"Whatever," I mumbled, no longer in a good mood.

Zion must have noticed my shift in attitude. She walked over to the candy aisle, "Chocolate bar?" she offered with a grin on her face. It had been the running joke ever since we were younger, considering how we met.

"Very funny," I responded.

We roamed the aisles aimlessly until we were standing in front of a clothes rack.

"Oh my gosh," Zion exclaimed, holding up a gray jacket, "this would look so good on you!"

She handed me the wool lined gray hoodie. I unzipped the jacket and slipped my arms into their appropriate holes. After adjusting the jacket, I zipped myself in. It was ridiculously comfortable. Rather than get my hopes up, I looked at the price tag. I knew it was too good to be true. I immediately removed the hoodie and placed it back on the hanger.

"What's wrong?" Zion asked, blocking me from restocking the jacket.

"That's way outside of my budget. I don't have $40 to spend on a hoodie." I answered, still trying to hang the jacket back on its rack.

Zion gave me a wink and grabbed the hanger from my hand, "That's why I'm buying it. You've been working so hard. You deserve a treat."

My thoughts were interrupted by my mother's screeching, "Charity, it's time for school! If you want a ride then you had better get down here, now!"

I heeded my mother's warning and ran down the steps. We didn't speak much on the car ride to school, but that had become the norm over the last three or four years. My mind was always wondering about Zion and who even knows what my mom was thinking about. She pulled up to the front of Chamberlain High and stopped the car. This was unusual. She usually stalled long enough for me to hop out and then sped off. But not this morning, this morning she decided to offer some "motherly advice".

Reaching over and placing her hand on my forearm, "For God's sake Charity, take off that awful hoodie! You're hiding all of your best parts."

Typical.

"Thanks mom," I responded, rolling my eyes. I hopped out of the car and immediately put the hood over my head and walked towards the entrance. The way I felt today I wanted to hide all of my parts.

I saw Amina and Tiana chatting near the entrance and I waved. Amina waved back, but I could see the scowl on Tiana's face plain and clear. As soon as Tiana saw me, she grabbed Amina's arm and they darted into the building. I followed. I had never really liked Amina's friends. There was something very sneaky about the both of them. Tiana could be civil at times, but whenever she got around Kendra, she was a different person.

Speak of the devil...

"Are you heading to stalk Amina some more?" Kendra asked from behind me. She sped up her pace until she was beside me and gave me a light shove towards the lockers.

"Leave me alone Kendra," I said, catching my balance. Kendra was now in front of me. I continued to trail behind Amina and Tiana.

"You know, this little weird lesbian crush thing you have going on is not cool," Kendra teased, "Plus, Amina doesn't even like you as a friend, so you should really back off!"

Kendra's words could be very hurtful, but I had learned to ignore them over the years. I kept my pace and was only a few steps behind Kendra when I felt someone tap my shoulder.

"Nice jacket," the voice complimented.

I turned around and was face to face with one of the cutest boys I had ever seen in my sixteen years of life.

"Thanks," I responded. My bottom lip got caught on my braces, but I talked through the pain, "It was a gift from a friend."

The handsome boy leaned in so close that I could smell his cologne, "I know."

He winked and I giggled; I never giggle.

"And how do you know that?" I asked.

"Because I bought it, silly." was his response.

I raised an eyebrow at him. I looked him over once more but was sure I'd never seen him before. Plus, I know who bought my hoodie. Wait…

"Zion?" I paused for a response. The handsome boy nodded.

I threw my hands around his neck, "Man, am I happy to see you," I punched his arm lightly, "I thought you were flirting with me. What's with the new look?"

He grinned, "I think you and I need to talk, somewhere private."

I was so happy to see her that I didn't care that she was now a he. Personally, I couldn't wait to hear the explanation.

"Let's do that. Just give me a second to go and wash my hands and then we can get out of here."

I walked towards the restroom. Despite how happy I was to see Zion, I needed to check in on Amina. Something didn't feel right. My gut was correct; the door to the girl's restroom was locked. I lightly tapped on the door, hoping I wasn't too late. Nothing happened, so I tapped again. When Amina answered the door, unharmed, I breathed a sigh of relief. Her friends weren't very happy with her, which I could tell from the snarky comments they made as they exited the restroom. Now that I knew Amina was safe, we held a little small talk, I washed my hands, and then I made my way back to Zion. She, well he was waiting at the front door of the school.

"Where are we going?" I asked.

"I know a perfect spot, not too far from here." he shared.

We walked away from the school until we reached a trail in the woods beside the football field. We hadn't gotten too far when he stated we had reached our destination. As a matter of fact, I could still see the stadium lights above the football field peeking over the trees.

"You've really got a thing for creepy buildings," I joked.

He smiled, "Best way to keep things quiet."

We walked in and he turned on the lights. Two chairs sat in the middle of the room and I remembered the first day I met Zion.

"And now the two chairs? Have you been taking a walk down memory lane?" I teased.

"I have. Since you brought it up, let's play a game about our memories," he suggested.

"I'm fine with that," I responded. I wasn't sure where this was going, but Zion was a quirky individual so I went with it.

He asked me to sit in the chair and close my eyes. Soon I felt rope being tied around my wrists. He quickly tied my legs to the chair as well. I guess we were going straight into training, which was fine because I was feeling a little rusty after two years of nothing. When he put the gag in my mouth, I became concerned. How can I answer questions if I can't speak? A few moments went by and I heard him dragging something into the chair beside me.

"Open your eyes, Amina." he commanded.

My heart almost beat out of my chest. He had called me Amina. Zion NEVER called me Amina during training; it always felt silly since we knew the truth. My body tensed up and I immediately knew this was not a test. This was real.

I opened my eyes and was face to face with the handsome boy who had seemed so harmless only minutes before. The sinister grin on his handsome face frightened me as he pointed to the chair beside me. I turned my head to look at what he was pointing to. Involuntarily, I let out a blood-curdling wail.

Sitting beside me was Zion, well what was left of her. She was still alive, but barely so. We didn't have to speak for me to know where she had been for the last two years. I wanted to see her again, but not like this.

He walked over and ran his fingers through her matted hair. Grabbing a fistful, he lifted her head, "Is this the Zion that you were looking for?" he taunted.

I did not respond. I refused to give him the satisfaction.

He shrugged, "I guess it isn't."

Walking towards a table that was near the door to the building, he grabbed a hammer. He strolled leisurely back towards our chairs, whistling a disturbing tune. "So if this is not your Zion, then it won't matter when I do this."

He lifted the hammer above his head. The gag was fitted so tightly that I didn't have time to object. My eyes screamed for him to stop, but it was too late. He proceeded to strike Zion in the face over and over again until nothing was left, but a bloody, pulpy mess. I looked away and resigned myself to my fate. He thought I was Amina, and I planned to keep it that way.

He began to rant and rave about feeling invisible, but all I could think about was Zion. The tears began to fall from my eyes and I couldn't control it. At one point he even lowered my gag. I attempted to scream for help, but it was all for show. I knew that no one could save me. Squirming in my chair, I struggled with the ropes around my wrists. I wanted to be free so badly. I knew my only hope of escape would be if I killed this awful thing that had taken my friend away. But the ropes were too tight. I was trapped.

My mind was blank. I waited for him to end my suffering, but he continued to talk about memories and torture. What I hadn't expected was for him to taste my blood. I never fully understood why I was getting the blood infusions, until now. The freak seemed to have liked what he tasted because he didn't miss a beat as he continued to talk about taking my power. Little did he know I had trained for this; I would die with the secret.

The murderer continued to ask questions that I would not answer. I could see the frustration settling in due to my lack of cooperation. I knew this was it for me. I took a deep breath and prayed that I would see Zion on the other side.

For a brief moment, a thought popped into my head. Could this all be a test? Maybe *this* was the ultimate test. Maybe that heap of dead flesh beside me wasn't real at all. Maybe she was just waiting to jump out and let me know I passed with flying colors. The possibility gave me hope and for a fleeting moment, I was happy. And then I felt his nails drag across my throat.

My job was done.

The Night Prince will always prevail! I had always known I was destined for greatness, but today I would finally prove it. Thanks to her little friend, Zion, I was able to spot her in the crowd very easily. It took two years for the Guardian to crack so I thought finding the girl in the gray hoodie would be a much more tedious task.

"We knew that finding the girl would be easy! We told you it would be easy!"

The voices had been correct right this time.

I dropped the blood-soaked hammer to the ground and kicked over the chair that supported Zion's lifeless body. Killing her had never been a part of my plan, but the voices said I had to. The smell of death was radiating from the corpse, so I reached into my back pocket and lay what was left of a dying rose on Zion's chest.

I shifted my attention back to my prize. The look of surprise on her face amused me, "Have you ever felt invisible? You know, I didn't know just how invisible I was, until I wasn't," releasing a sigh of relief, I stretched my arms into the air, "It feels so good to be free!"

The girl in the gray hoodie stared back at me with tear-filled eyes. I lowered the gag to grant her speech. At the very least, she deserved to speak her peace.

"Help me!" she screamed, "Somebody, help me!"

"Silence her! She will not be missed. Tell her! Tell her she will not be missed!"

I shook my head at her feigned attempt at escape and immediately placed the gag back in her mouth, "No one can hear you. Look around. No one even knows you are missing!"

I laughed thinking of how easy it was to lure her. I had always imagined that she would be a much prettier girl, but her lack of beauty worked to my advantage. Like a baby starved for attention, she hung on my every word and gladly followed me to this abandoned building. The room lacked natural light due to the boards on the windows, but I didn't need the light to see the fear in her eyes.

I dragged the nail of my little finger across her cheek and watched the small droplets of blood formulate. My attempts to look away failed and I found myself licking the side of her face, "Mmmm," a moan escaped from my lips, "I taste the power inside of you." Involuntarily, I licked her face again, "The more I taste, the more I learn. I know who you were, who you are, and who you would have become."

"We must have her!"

"Let me think!" I shouted. I needed a clear head to try and break the girl. The tears streaming down her face added fuel to my fire. The savory taste of fear had always stimulated my appetite. I licked my lips imagining how fulfilled I would be when this was over, "Would you like to know what I'm thinking little girl?"

She did not respond.

"The girl mocks you with her silence!"

They were right again, but I would not give them the satisfaction. Ignoring the voices, I continued my tease, "I will take your lack of objection as a yes. First, I am going to steal your memories; I need to know everything, especially about the others."

She did not react.

I covered my ears as I heard the voices all laugh in unison.

"You call yourself the Night Prince, but you are weak. You can rule no one! Even the girl does not fear you!"

I ran my fingers down her back and walked them back up along her spine, "Then, I am going to peel your flesh off, bit by bit. Now, I will need you alive for this part. I can't wait to see how long you last before passing out."

She flinched.

"Who's weak now?" I cackled to the demons inside of me. Their silence pleased me. Now to get on with it. She had flinched, I was breaking her down.

"Ahhh, you didn't like that part, did you? Well, then you definitely won't like the end. I think that the only way for me to guarantee that you are actually dead is to swallow you whole. Plus," I patted my contorting gut, "I have some friends that want to meet you."

She squirmed in her chair, but there was no escape.

"Struggling only makes the flesh more tender," I whispered in her ear.

The light in her eyes dimmed and I made my way to her side. Pressing my palms to her temples, I prepared to take her memories once again. The memories began to flood into my mind quickly. I watched her grow old, and then young again. I saw the beginning of time and the end of time, all through her eyes. My heart began to race when I saw the Innocents and then all of a sudden, the memories vanished. I pressed harder, but there was nothing.

"She defies us! Kill her!"

"Keeping some for yourself, are we?" I probed, "If you don't want to play nice then I won't either."

I dug my nails into her temples. She didn't even blink. Still pressing her temples, I felt the empty feeling of the memories fading away.

"KILL THE GIRL! KILL THE GIRL! KILL THE GIRL!"

The voices won, "I don't have time for this," I slid my nails across her throat and watched the blood rush down her blouse. Removing the gag to listen to her gurgle on her own blood, I laid my head in her lap. Now fully immersed in the plunge pool of the waterfall that her blood was creating, I could taste the hints of the power that I craved. The thought of having her inside of me was overwhelming. I cracked my bottom jaw so that I could enjoy this scrumptious treat in one bite. After years of searching, she would be mine!

"Give her to us!"

I obeyed. In one fell swoop, the task was complete. I fell back onto the ground and awaited my new body. The form of a 16-year-old human girl was not my vision of power, but the Fates are funny that way. I could feel the transformation nearing its completion, but I noticed that I could no longer feel the power. I closed my eyes to view the memories, but again they were gone. All that remained were the silly memories of a 16-year-old girl named Charity.

Of course!

I should have known she was Hidden. I would have to be subtler next time. The Hidden were always the hardest to catch. I picked a sinewy mass from my teeth and threw it to the ground. The girl in the gray hoodie was just a cloak! On the bright side, if this was her cloak, then she couldn't be far. I smiled as I made my way back to the high school in my new form. Again, I stopped at the bush to pick a flower. I inhaled the essence of the rose and stashed it in my pocket.

I'll keep this body…for now.

CHAPTER 7: THE WOMAN IN WHITE

"The cloak is down!" the young man shouted over the intercom, "I repeat the cloak is down!"

Guardian's Groceries was buzzing with energy. The headquarters had never prepared the young man for this day. An older man ran into the room and shut the door behind him.

"Initiate protocol 500" the older man commanded.

"But sir," the younger of the two objected.

The older man grabbed the young man by his shirt and glared at his nametag, "Don't but sir, me, Private. Initiate protocol 500!"

The young man stood firm in his opinion, "Sir, with all due respect her memory is already fried. She ran back an entire decade! If I try to wipe her memory now, her brain may never recover."

The older man was now inches from the younger man's face, "Should I be taking commands from you, Private Willis? Or is it the other way around? I will only tell you one more time before I end your career, initiate protocol 500!"

Private Willis hung his head in defeat, "Yes sir. Protocol 500 has been initiated."

Just stay calm Amina. The words were repeatedly playing in my head as I shifted on the cold, restroom floor.

+2046598265

Will you help me Amina?

9:50am

Me

Who is this?

9:51am

I was still locked in the restroom, where I had been sitting

for the last 15 minutes, waiting for a response to the weird text

message I had received. For someone who seemed to need help,

the mystery person had no intentions of clueing me in.

KNOCK, KNOCK, KNOCK.

I could hear someone trying to push through the restroom

door. This was the third person attempting to enter with no

success. Listening to their frustration on the other side of the door,

I realized I needed to pull myself together. There was absolutely nothing I could do to figure out what was happening to me sitting on the floor in the girl's restroom. Grabbing the edge of the sink, I pulled myself to my feet. Now that I was faced with my distorted reflection again I immediately felt the urge to look away, but something caught my eye. Something I had not seen when I saw myself this morning. I leaned in closer to the mirror and tugged at the neckline of my sweater. I lowered it just enough to see my collarbone.

"You've got to be kidding me," I mumbled. I ran my fingers across the inflamed scar that sat at the intersection of my collarbone and the top of my left shoulder. The scar was linear and sunken in. I don't recall this being here before. The time to investigate this new wound would have to be later.

KNOCK, KNOCK, KNOCK.

"IS ANYONE IN HERE?" someone yelled from the other side of the door.

Person number four was banging on the door, with hopes of entering the restroom but unlike the others, this one sounded mad.

I quickly fixed my shirt, grabbed my things, and unlocked the door. There was no point in drawing unwanted attention, so I needed to walk out of here like everything was absolutely normal.

Deep breath.

I swung the door open, "Can't a girl get 5 minutes to herself?" I exclaimed, hoping I sounded as convincing as I needed to.

"Sorry, I really had to go." the freckled girl announced as she dashed around me and into the restroom.

I chuckled at her candor. This girl didn't care who I was nor how convincing I was; she just *really* had to pee. I left her and the restroom behind me to try and figure out the rest of this day.

I must have wandered aimlessly down the halls for an hour, hoping that something would spark a memory from a dream and I could find my way to class. Unfortunately, I was getting nowhere fast. Eventually, I found myself standing in front of the library. I guess this was as good a place as any to gather my thoughts. I strolled in and sat at a secluded table in the back. Only ten minutes had gone by when I started to feel like someone was watching me. Attempting to redirect my attention, I began scrolling through nonsense on my phone, but I couldn't shake the feeling. In the end, fear won the battle; I grabbed my things and moved to a new table.

Now that I felt a little less creeped out, I decided to put my phone to good use. I began to search for information on dreams and time traveling. The more I read, the more I started to feel like I had déjà vu. I couldn't put my finger on it, but everything about this moment felt strangely familiar. Unfortunately for me, my search was not necessarily fruitful. There were a few interesting perspectives on what could be happening, but for the most part, the internet is just filled with crazies. While bookmarking some pages to read later, I started to get that feeling again; the feeling that someone was watching me. Almost immediately there was a shadow cast over my phone screen.

Someone was watching me.

"What are you looking at?" the voice asked from above me.

I looked up to see Tiana standing over me and actively trying to view my search history.

"Nothing T," I lied, quickly placing my phone in my pocket, "How long have you been in here?"

She dropped her backpack to the ground and joined me at the table, "Not long. What happened to you in World History? Ms. Marshall is pissed that you skipped."

I made a mental note: World History with Ms. Marshall.

"I wasn't feeling well this morning. I just left the restroom not too long ago," I answered. It was a mostly true statement.

She held her nose and waved her free hand in front of her face, "I guess I'll be going to the restroom on the second floor after lunch."

"Hahaha," I deadpanned, "I was just getting my thoughts together, nothing major." I wanted to change the subject, "Where are you headed to anyway? What made you stop in here?"

She shrugged, "I don't know. I just had this feeling you were in here, and I was right! Isn't that funny? I can always sniff you out."

She was telling the truth.. I had noticed pretty early out in my dreams that Tiana *ALWAYS* knew where I was. It was weird.

"Most people don't brag about being expert stalkers," I joked with her.

We laughed until the Librarian shot menacing looks in our direction. Tiana stuck her tongue out at the lady and turned her attention back to me.

"Well now that I've found you let's go to lunch." She stood up and looked around, "This library creeps me out."

"Me too," I stated, gathering my belongings.

We were almost in the hallway when I heard someone call my name. The voice was coming from inside the library. "Amina, someone left this book behind for you."

I couldn't make out who the person was that was shouting at me was from where I was standing in the hallway, but I figured it was the Librarian.

"One second," I said to Tiana.

Walking back into the Library, I began to feel a little dizzy. The spinning got worse with every step I took, and it was too much to bear seconds before I reached the Librarian's desk. I quickly grabbed the edge of the desk to keep myself from falling. The Librarian placed her hand over mine to steady me.

"Everything ok, Amina?" she questioned.

I nodded without looking up. My equilibrium was back to normal, but I still felt strange. It felt like my entire body was on fire. I noticed the woman's hand was still resting on mine so I pulled my hand back in case she could feel the inferno that was building underneath my skin. The moment our hands were apart, my body temperature dropped back to normal.

"Here's the book you requested," she said while shoving a book in my face.

I grabbed the book and read the title: *The Age of the Innocents.* Strange title. I flipped the book over to read the back cover, but there was nothing there except worn leather. There must be a reason that I had placed this on hold. I made a mental note to read through the book tonight. Maybe it will give me a clue to what is going on or how to get out of this dream.

"Thanks!" I said, finally looking up at the Librarian.

I walked away with the image of the Librarian etched into my brain. I couldn't help but feel like I had seen her somewhere before. I had made it back to Tiana in the hallway when it hit me. That's the same rude woman from the bus that bumped into me this morning! Since my dreams were allowing me to have a little power these days, I decided to march back into the Library to confront the woman about her behavior this morning.

Hands on hips, I turned the corner and approached the desk, ready to give her a piece of my mind. I took a deep breath and prepared to tell her off, but she was gone. An older, frail woman with horn-rimmed glasses sat in her place. I continued my march to the desk anyway. I figure this woman must be her superior.

"Where is the woman that just gave me this book?" I asked, thrusting the book into the frail woman's face.

The woman stared at me like I was crazy, "What woman?" she asked, thumbing through the book.

I rolled my eyes, "The woman who just gave me this book!" I repeated.

The frail woman scowled, "Are you high?"

I laughed, "What does that have to do with anything? And for the record, no I am not high."

The woman stood up and looked me square in the eyes, "Your eyes look a little glossy to me."

By this point I was beyond annoyed.

"Ma'am, can you please just tell me where the woman went who gave me this book? She is my complexion with long, jet black hair. She had on a white dress." I questioned her again.

"Young lady, I have been sitting at this desk for the past hour. I watched you walk in, change tables, and then leave without checking out a single book. Plus, this book is not even one of ours." she said pushing the book back into my hands. "I will not tolerate substance abuse in my library! You need to leave now before I contact administration."

I was not prepared to explain anything to anyone, especially not an administrator. My feet made their way to the exit, even though my brain was still waiting for answers. I ran into the hall, searching for Tiana and we almost collided.

"Where did you go?" I asked.

"To get some water," she pointed at the nearby fountain, "What about you? That took way longer than a second." Tiana glanced at her watch sarcastically.

I chose to ignore her dig. I needed to be sure I wasn't going completely insane, "You saw her didn't you?"

"Saw who?" she asked, walking in what I assumed was the direction of the cafeteria.

"That woman! The woman in the white dress in the library. The one who handed me this." I said while pointing to the book.

Tiana studied the book, "I've seen that before." She grabbed the book from me and ran her fingers down its spine, "I think I saw it in a dream I had the other night."

Hearing the word dream, my ears started buzzing and my heart began to race. The look on Tiana's face did not help the situation either. Tiana continued to stare at the book, and it seemed like she was in a trance. She didn't blink, she didn't speak, and I wasn't even sure if she was still breathing.

"Tiana," I shouted, snapping my fingers in her face.

She scrunched up her face and threw the book back in my direction, "Oh yeah, sorry. I started thinking about that weird dream I had the other night. But anyway, of course I saw that woman in the Library. You're talking about the one with the long hair, right? I absolutely loved her dress. Do you think I could pull off an all-white ensemble?"

I nodded and released a sigh of relief. I couldn't be crazy if Tiana had seen her too, right? I followed Tiana to the into the line for pizza. She was still talking about the woman in white.

"Although she was extremely fashionable, to be honest, she was the one giving me the creeps. Seriously Amina, when I walked in, she was staring at you like she wanted to eat you."

My thoughts were going a mile a minute. So the disappearing woman was the one watching me the whole time I was in there? If she was in there, then why did the frail Librarian lie? What if the woman in white is the weirdo that's been texting my phone? What if she knows why I'm stuck in this dream?

Tiana continued to speak, oblivious to the fact that my mind was in another place, "Yep, I think she wanted to eat you about as much as I want to eat this pizza." She grabbed two slices of pizza, placing one on her plate and the other on an empty plate that she handed to me. "Are you hungry?"

I forced my racing thoughts into the shadows of my mind and grabbed the plate, "Let's eat."

When we emerged from the line, I spotted Kendra waving us over to a table. We were almost at the table with Kendra, when I bumped into Charity. Our bodies were in contact for less than a second, but in that split second my body's natural defenses went into overdrive. The hair stood up on the back of my neck and I was covered in goosebumps. She had been walking pretty fast, so the force of the collision knocked the orange juice she was holding to the ground.

"Sorry, Charity," I said picking up the juice. I offered the juice back to her and she quickly snatched it away.

"Whatever," she grumbled. I guess she hadn't realized that I was the person that bumped into her. When she looked up at my face, she smiled, "Oh, I didn't know it was you *Amina*."

Something about the way she said my name made me uncomfortable. I brushed it off, "You want to come and eat with us?" I asked still trying to shake the feeling. I pointed to the table that Tiana and Kendra were sitting at a few feet away.

She didn't answer me. She just kept staring and smiling. Maybe this is why we stopped hanging out? I frantically rubbed my arm, trying to get rid of the goosebumps, but it wasn't working.

"Charity?" I questioned.

The smile on her face disappeared and she became nervous, "Uh, no…you know they don't really like me. I think I'll just go be by myself."

She didn't give me a chance to rebuttal. I watched Charity walk away and she never looked back. I couldn't put my finger on it, but even she seemed different from this morning. This is weird. I checked my phone, hoping that I still had Charity's number saved. Thankfully, it was still saved in my phone. I sent her a text to see what was up. She responded quickly and from the looks of it everything was normal, at least with her. I finally made it to the table with Kendra and Tiana, and I took a seat. All of this craziness was affecting my appetite. I am starving! I don't think anyone likes cafeteria food, but on this day school lunch pizza was giving me life!

"What was that all about?" Kendra asked, digging into a salad.

"What are you talking about?" Tiana redirected.

Kendra pointed at me, "I'm talking to Amina. What was with that little blow-off from your friend? Usually, she won't stop talking your ear off."

I shrugged, "I have no idea." This was one of the most honest things I had said all day.

Tiana changed the subject and before long I was enjoying lunch. Reminiscing with my two best friends reminded me of why I loved them so much. On a day like today when I couldn't figure out my left from right, lunch with two good friends was all I needed to feel grounded.

After watching a few people throw away their trash, I decided to act like a normal student and take my plate to the disposal station. I was placing my plate down when I felt someone standing a little too close behind me. Playing it cool, I spun around on my heels, hoping to catch the creep in action. I was now inches away from the woman in the white dress from the Library.

"Read the book." She whispered.

Startled, I jumped back.

And then she vanished.

I mean she literally vanished right before my eyes…and then I fainted.

⁎⁎

A day in the life of a teenage nobody had started off less than pleasant.

Being trapped in this body would take some getting used to. Nonetheless, this sorry sack of flesh was doing its job. I bumped into *her* today. She spoke to me as if we were friends. If that were the case, then it would only make this easier. I kept trying to pull information about the powerful one from the cloak's memory, but anything related to Amina had been wiped. I was going to have to figure this out on my own.

The cloak's pocket vibrated. Apparently, Charity had received a text:

Amina

Everything ok?

12:50pm

"They are friends. Killing the girl will be easy!"

For once they were pleased. I tuned out their celebration while I struggled to think of a response. I pulled from the teenage memories that Charity's soul provided to come up with a response that would make sense:

Me

Sorry. That time of the month.

12:51pm

Amina

Kk. Well, text me if you need to talk.

12:52pm

Me

I will.

12:53pm

I placed the phone back in the scraggly girl's pocket and wandered down the hall with so much hope that I didn't notice the group of boys pointing and laughing ahead of me. While shuffling past them towards my designated class, someone tripped me. I fell to the ground, dropping all of my schoolbooks. When I looked up, I saw the group of cocky human males laughing. Their jackets signified that they were apart of some sort of school team.

"The homeless shelter is that way!" the largest in the group sneered, pointing outside of the school doors.

"Everyone thinks you are weak. Show them who you are! KILL HIM!"

I had to stay focused, "Not yet," I mumbled to silence the voices.

"Who are you talking to, freak?" the large one asked, slapping my books out of my hand again. He snorted with laughter and slapped fives with his friends.

I quickly gathered my things. Before walking away, I reached into my back pocket and handed the large one the rose I had picked earlier. He didn't know how to respond to the gesture,

but he eventually crushed the rose in his palm. I walked away

without saying a word. I never forget a face; his time would come.

CHAPTER 8: THE MESSAGE

I ran up the stairs with confidence and made my way to the exposed railing.

"Kendra, I really can fly, watch!" I yelled.

Climbing on top of the rail, I balanced the soles of my feet to prepare for dismount.

From where I was standing, I could see Kendra staring up at me intently waiting for me to fly. I removed the scrunchie from my wrist and carefully ran my fingers through my thick curly hair and wrapped it tightly in a ponytail. I felt the A/C kick on, and a slight breeze began to blow through the house. The wind caught the bottom of my white, satin nightgown and I basked in the moment.

"Here I go!" I said, spreading my arms out beside me. The world seemed to freeze the moment I leapt from the banister. For just a second, I was gliding like a beautiful dove. But the peace I felt in that second quickly diminished when I felt someone or something push me. I began to panic. My eyes locked on Kendra's as we both noticed that I was not going to land on the couch. I saw Kendra's eyes fill with concern and from nowhere a gust of wind pushed me back towards the couch. I plummeted into the cushions and said a silent prayer of thanks to the A/C.

"THAT WAS AWESOME!" I screamed, jumping from the couch, "Did you see me fly?"

Kendra stood in shock for a moment but didn't say a word.

I ran up to Kendra and grabbed her hands, "Did you see me?"

"I saw you." A voice whispered from the shadows.

I walked towards the shadowed corner of the room, but reality pulled me back. When I woke up, I was in the nurse's office.

"How are you feeling Ms. Wallace?" the nurse questioned.

Her back was turned, but I noticed the long black hair right away. I tried to lift myself up to get a better look, but I couldn't. My head was spinning again, so I laid back down.

"Don't try to get up. You hit your head pretty hard in the cafeteria," she informed.

I listened closely to her voice. Immediately, I could feel my temperature rising again. I knew that this was not the nurse. No, this was the woman in white. The same woman from the bus, the library, and the cafeteria. I must be losing my mind.

"Who are you?" I asked hesitantly.

She did not turn around, but she did answer, "A friend."

I waited for her to say something, anything more, but she didn't.

"Why are you following me?" I questioned.

Backing up slowly, she turned around. She then lowered her face to mine until we were eye to eye, "I'm not the only one that is following you, little girl."

"W-What are you talking about?" I stammered.

She shook her head in disappointment, "I've watched you every day, and you never saw me. I know everything there is to know about you, but you never saw me. And now here we are, face to face. It's too late to be afraid, Amina. Do you see me now?"

She placed her hand on the scar and I felt an immediate burning sensation in my shoulder. It was the same feeling I felt in the Library earlier today.

"What are you doing to me?" I shouted.

The burning sensation was increasing, but she did not remove her hand. I attempted to move my shoulder, but my body refused to cooperate.

"Do you see me?" she questioned.

With her eyes were still locked on mine. She lifted her hand, and the burning stopped.

"You don't see a thing, do you? Tell me Amina, how old do you think you are?" she asked.

I wasn't sure of what she what she thought she knew, but I wasn't going to out myself. "I don't know," I said.

Her face contorted and she continued to shake her head, "Do you remember who I am?"

I thought long and hard, but I couldn't come up with an answer. I shook my head, "I've never met you before today."

She placed her hand on my forehead and closed her eyes, "Wow. They really did a number on your memory. It's alright. I'm going to help you."

I didn't trust this strange woman with the burning touch, "Who are you?" I asked for the second time.

She smiled, "My name is Marlena."

I had heard that name before.

As the name, Marlena echoed in my head I remembered where I had seen her face before. She was in my room the night I fell into this dream. She was the woman that emerged from the light.

"I saw you!" I yelled, "Why am I here? Get me out of this dream!"

Her eyes lowered, "Even if this were a dream, I can't."

The room began to vibrate. The woman in white began to fade away, but before she completely disappeared I saw a hand the color of night cover her mouth and pull her away. She was gone, but the room was still shaking. I shut my eyes tightly as the room started to spin again.

I must have fainted again. When I opened my eyes, I was still in the nurse's office, but this time there was no woman with long black hair to greet me.

"Are you feeling any better Ms. Wallace?" the gray-haired nurse asked me.

I ignored her first question, "What happened to me?" It felt like my head had a bandage on it.

"You fell pretty hard in the cafeteria. Did you slip on something?" she prodded.

I shook my head yes, afraid that they would cart me off to the loony bin if I told the truth.

She began to unwrap the bandage on my head, "Just a small nick. Nothing a little rubbing alcohol and Neosporin won't cure." She pressed a moist cotton ball to my forehead. The stinging sensation indicated that this was the previously mentioned rubbing alcohol. She then grabbed a tube of Neosporin and applied it to a bandage, "Would you like me to apply this darling?"

"No ma'am, I can do it." I said while standing up. Surprisingly, I was able to stand with ease. I politely grabbed the bandage and made my way to the mirror. As I was placing the bandage on my forehead, I realized how red my collar bone was. And then, I remembered the burning sensation.

"Marlena," I mumbled.

The nurse chuckled, "Yeah, you were saying something about a Marlena in your sleep. It must have been one heck of a dream. You were tossing and turning all over the place!"

I tuned out her rambling and ran my fingers along the scar.

I looked back at the nurse who was still rambling about my dreams, "You kept saying 'my pocket, my pocket, my pocket' over and over again. And then you finally just woke up."

I forced a smile, "I must have hit my head pretty hard. Thanks for taking care of me!" I slid my hand into my pocket and felt a crumbled piece of paper. I needed to get out of here. I headed out of the nurse's office and found myself in an empty hallway. Empty, all except for one person, Charity. She saw me before I could approach.

"Hi Amina." she waved.

I waved back. She seemed to be in a much better mood than she had been in the cafeteria, but I did not have time to talk to her. I needed to figure out what had happened to the woman in the white dress. I made a point to walk in the opposite direction, but Charity followed behind me anyway.

"Are you feeling okay? I saw you coming out of the nurse's office," she asked once she had caught up.

My mind flashed to the image of the scraggly little girl I had met years ago at the therapy sessions and I stopped. We were apparently real friends once upon a time, so I could at least talk to her.

I pointed to the bandage, "Watch your step in the cafeteria."

Her eyes focused on my forehead. She rummaged through her backpack before speaking, "Looks like you need a fresh bandage. That one is bleeding through." Leaning in, she peeled the bloody bandage from my head and applied the new one.

"That's gross!" I squealed when I saw the bloody mess that she was holding, "Give it to me, I'll throw that away." I reached, but she pulled her hand back.

"Don't worry. I'll get rid of it. I was headed to the restroom either way," she said revealing her now blood-stained palms.

"You look like you just killed someone with your bare hands," I responded.

Charity snorted, "Now that would be ridiculous. Look, I'll catch up with you later. I need to wash my hands."

She smiled and scurried off.

I shouted behind her, "Thanks, Charity! You have no idea how helpful you've been today."

I watched her walk away, wondering what memories we shared. I can't imagine why we would have stopped being friends. My trip down memory lane was cut short when my ears tuned into the click-clack of heels against the laminate.

Kendra.

"You are starting to hang out with her more than me." she stated with a twinge of an attitude in her voice.

"Don't start, Kendra," I sighed, "I'm clearly having a bad day."

Kendra locked her arm in mine, "Yeah, Humpty-Dumpty, I saw you hit the floor face first. You haven't been drinking have you?"

Instinctively, I referenced the dream I had in the nurse's office, "I would never drink a drop without you, dear."

She laughed and we walked down the hall reminiscing on the memory.

"You really thought that you could fly!" she teased.

I shook my head in shame, "Yeah, and my couch still has the sunken in cushion to prove it. Thank goodness I didn't land on the hardwood floors; I probably would've broken all of my bones."

She nodded in agreement with a sly grin on her face, "Now if only we can figure out who pushed you to safety?"

"I think we have the A/C to thank for that," I answered.

Kendra released my arm, "Seriously, Amina?"

I had no idea what I had done, "What?"

"Nothing," she huffed, placing her hand on my forehead, "how hard did you fall?"

I had to recover. I wasn't sure what I had done, but Kendra seemed a bit put off. I changed the subject, "So how's your dad?" Kendra's mom had passed many years after the divorce and her dad was not the easiest man to get along with.

She rolled her eyes, "That womanizer is lucky I still claim him," she did a spin and her yellow sundress danced in the breeze, "but he does keep me in designer clothes, so I guess he can stay."

Kendra had always been the epitome of chic. She had the body of a model and the brains of a Physicist. Standing 5'10" tall, her skin resembled a natural Umber pigmentation with warm golden undertones. Her coffee-bean colored, naturally wavy hair fell right below her shoulders. In a word, she was stunning!

"You two are perfect for one another. The womanizer and the spoiled daughter, I think I've seen that movie on Lifetime." I jabbed. I interlocked my arm with hers again before we continued our walk. Something about being so close to her felt safe.

"I have a question for you Kendra. Do you ever remember seeing Charity at any of the meetings we used to go to?"

Kendra rolled her eyes, "Nope, but you always said you did. I thought it was funny that she was never there when I was, but she made you comfortable so whatever. Why do you ask?"

"Just wondering," A sharp pain shot into my shoulder. I tugged at the neckline of my sweater attempting to alleviate the burning sensation.

"Wait a minute," she said, pulling away again, "What's wrong with your neck?" She placed her index finger on my collar bone and traced the inflamed area, "What happened to your birthmark?"

"Birthmark?" I questioned. This wasn't a birthmark. I had never even seen this scar until today.

Kendra raised an eyebrow at me, "Are you sure we don't need to take you to the hospital for a CT scan? How did you forget your own birthmark?" She reached back up to touch the scar, well, birthmark. Her touch was like a cool compress and the burning sensation I had felt before was a distant memory. Thinking about the burning sensation reminded me of the note that was in my pocket. Between the note I had yet to read and this so-called birthmark, I really needed to be alone to gather my thoughts.

I pulled away, "Look, I've got to go. But let's catch up later, ok?"

She looked at me with those deep brown eyes and I felt like she was staring a hole in me, "What really happened to your neck, Amina?" she asked again.

I waved off her concern, "I don't know. It must have happened during the fall. But I feel much better now!" I began to walk towards the exit of the school, hoping I would be in time to catch the bus home, "You should really consider becoming a masseuse!" I yelled as I walked out of the school doors.

I looked back and saw her still standing there staring at me through the doors. I hated for her to be worried about me, but I needed to read this note. I pulled the note out of my pocket and smoothed it out:

Don't trust anyone—not even yourself!

And read the book, especially the first three chapters.

-M

I crumpled the note and placed it back in my pocket. I had almost forgotten about the book. Kneeling on the ground, I searched my backpack for the book the dream woman handed me in the Library. If I still had the book, then maybe she was real. But if she was real, then what the hell is going on? I dug around for a few more seconds and I felt the spine of a book in my hand. I pulled it out only to see that it was my Geometry book. I guess she wasn't real after all--but then who gave me this note?

"Looking for this?" I heard someone ask.

I had been so focused on looking for the book that I didn't hear the car pulling up beside me. I rose from the kneeled position and saw Tiana holding my book out of the passenger side of some guy's red Mustang. I ran over and grabbed the book.

"You dropped it in the cafeteria when you took that little tumble," she shared. She leaned out of the window and grabbed my shirt, "What happened to your birthmark?"

"This happened when I fell," I lied. I guess this was a birthmark after all, "Who's that?" I whispered, placing the book back in my backpack.

"No one special." she winked, settling back into the passenger seat.

The guy in the driver's seat mumbled something and pulled off before I could ask any more questions.

"You could have at least offered a ride," I shouted in the car's direction.

Walking over to the bus stop, I contemplated the events of the day. At this point, I wasn't sure if I was dreaming or not. If this is a dream, I can't even remember where I'm trying to get back to. Opening the book, I thumbed through the pages while I waited for the bus to arrive. Despite my efforts to read the words on the page, my mind was stuck on the woman in white. I guess the woman who called herself Marlena, was real. Well, I'm not sure if she is real, but she is definitely something. She did disappear like three times in one day, so maybe she's a ghost. I had finally focused enough to skim through pages of the book, with the hopes of finding some explanation for my day, when I heard a car stop in front of me.

"Need a ride?" Charity questioned, motioning for me to make my way over. For the second time today, I was taken aback by Charity's presence. She definitely seemed a bit off. In fact, she didn't even look like herself. Normally, I would have tried to figure out what was wrong, but I didn't have the time or energy to deal with anyone else's problems today.

"No, thank you," I answered, stuffing the book behind my back.

"What you got there?" she asked, peering out of her passenger window.

"Some reading for AP Literature," I lied, "It's a real snooze fest!" I responded, pretending to fall asleep at the bus stop.

She scrunched up her face and glanced in her backseat, "Well you have fun with that. I'll see you soon!"

I waved as she drove off in the tan minivan. I didn't remember her having a car, but I guess I didn't remember a lot of things these days. I focused my attention back on the book. Time to get some answers!

Bumping into Amina twice in one day was luck. I locked the restroom door behind me and stared at my blood stained hands. It was definitely her. I licked both of my hands, but it was not enough. I unwrapped the band aid and licked it clean as well. I had to have her now!

"We MUST have her!"

"I know, and we will," I responded.

I washed my hands and left the restroom. I needed to get out of this school and come up with a plan. Upon my exit, my eyes landed on the cocky human that had tripped me earlier. He was in the shaded area of the parking lot, so I headed in his direction.

"What do you want Charity?" he scoffed, digging in his pockets for his keys.

I looked around to make sure we were the only ones in the parking lot.

"Give him to us! We shall teach him a lesson!"

I lifted my shirt to reveal the beasts inside, ""I don't want anything, but they want your soul."

His eyes were glued to my distorted figure, and the color began to drain from his face. I loved the look of confusion that appeared on my victim's faces right before I ended them. Unhinging my jaw, I locked on to his neck and sunk my teeth into his pink, splotchy flesh. As the blood from the lacerations in his neck began to pour down my throat, I dragged his body inside the tan minivan. He had an unpleasant aftertaste, but I continued to drink. I would need all the strength I could find to take down Amina. Once he was nearly drained, I threw his backpack and football equipment on top of him to cover up the mess I had made.

I hopped in the driver's seat of his vehicle and was about to pull off when I saw Amina standing at a bus stop. I made sure to wipe the blood from my lips with the sleeve of the gray hoodie before offering her a ride. Thankfully, she wasn't interested. The voices hissed in anger as I drove away.

"You should have taken her!"

I'd had it with their demands. Slamming on the breaks, I stopped the car in the middle of the road. "It is your fault that I could not take her," I shouted! "Because of your impulsiveness, there is a body in the backseat. How could I have explained that?" My anger reached an uncontrollable level, and I was now hitting myself over and over again, "THIS IS ALL YOUR FAULT!" I screamed to the demons that lived inside of me.

When I heard the dying boy moan from his hiding spot, I snapped out of it. I needed to get out of here and get rid of him. The voices fell silent and I was finally able to drive in peace.

"Some other time, Amina Wallace. Some other time," I mumbled to myself, driving away from Chamberlain High.

CHAPTER 9: THE BOOK

I don't think I've ever been so happy to see a city bus. It felt like I had been waiting for what felt like hours. I glanced down at my watch. Apparently, it had only been thirty minutes. Either way, exhausted is on the lower end of the spectrum of how I'm feeling after today. I dropped my loose coins into the money slot next to the bus driver and located a seat.

"How's it going, Amina?" the bus driver asked with a gap-toothed grin.

I turned back to face the husky man and quickly scanned his name tag, "I'm hanging in there, Terrence."

He patted me on the back, "You're a strong girl, and this is just one day of many. Keep your head up!" He waved for me to sit so that he could pull off.

I guess I could take comfort in the fact that everyone I bumped into today seemed to like me. I made my way down the aisle, running my fingers over the tattered navy seats. I chose a seat near the back. Being that I was the only passenger, the bus ride home was silent. It wasn't long before the bus pulled up to my stop. I walked back up the aisle and waited for the doors to swing open, but they didn't.

Terrence cleared his throat, "You'll figure this out, Amina."

The whizzing sound of compressed air being released let me know that he had finally opened the doors. I looked out onto the street that I had apparently always lived on and exited the bus. Once on the ground, I turned around to wave Terrence goodbye.

The bus doors whizzed closed, and I watched the massive blue and white haven disappear around a corner. The beeping sound of an alarm on my phone drew my attention. I dug around in my purse and saw the words '**Dinner with mom**' flashing on the screen. I guess I wouldn't get any alone time after all.

The walk home was brief, but relaxing. Although I couldn't quite remember where I was supposed to be, I wasn't too unhappy that I was here. With each step, I felt more like this was where I needed to be. It felt nice to feel connected to something after spending an entire day in confusion; every crack on the sidewalk seemed to hold a memory, each streetlight reminded me of a scolding for coming home late, and even the light from the moon felt familiar. I think the dream might be over.

When I arrived at my front door, I hesitated. The confidence I was feeling during the walk home was diminishing. I pulled the crumpled note out of my pocket and read it one more time. Trust no one, not even myself. If I can't even trust myself then how would I ever know what was real and what wasn't? I put the note back in my pocket and opened the door. It was unlocked. I guess my mom was already home. I ran upstairs to place my things

in my room and get ready for dinner, but I found a note on my bed:

Can't do dinner tonight sweetie. Huge client called and

wants to meet. Next week?

-Love Mom

I flopped onto my bed with the book in hand. I guess this

life wasn't as glamorous as it seemed. I was stood up by my own

mom. However, this did provide the opportunity for me to delve

into this book.

"Well, here goes nothing," I mused aloud. I ran my palm

across the front cover of the leather-bound book. I wonder how old

this book is. Each crack in the leather seemed so deliberate.

"*The Age of the Innocents*" I read aloud.

I pried the book open slowly, afraid that whatever secrets it

held within its pages would attempt to escape. The brittle pages

had foxing around the edges. I had anticipated that the wrinkled

old pages would release a musty smell, but instead, a pleasant floral aroma greeted my nostrils. Handwriting on the endpaper caught my attention:

For the girl who lost her way. Always remember where you came from or else you will never know where you're going.

-M

I dropped the open book on my chest face down and stared at the ceiling thinking of how true her words were. Hopefully, this book would be my chance to find my way back to…well, me. Picking up the book, I flipped to the first chapter:

Chapter 1: The Promised Ones

The Age of Darkness was prophesied to end with the birth of The Innocents. The Innocents were to be formed in the wombs of the Sacred Souls. The Sacred Souls were three sisters that had survived a brutal witch hunt and were the last of a forgotten Coven. Per the prophecy, the three women would mate with a beast of the night to fulfill their destiny of delivering The Innocents to the realm.

The women traveled to the corners of the Universe to find the perfect specimens to empower the children. Marlena, the oldest of the three, had chosen to mate with a Kitsune. Kitsune were known for their ability to dream walk, fly, become invisible, and when angered or scared the Kitsune could emit fire or lightning.

Venus, the middle child, lay with a Gancanagh. This creature possessed the power of seduction. Though extremely narcissistic, the Gancanagh could make anyone fall for him. Venus was not won over by his charm, but she hoped his cunning intelligence and seductive prowess would benefit her child.

Lastly, Safina, the youngest, bred with an Encantado. This water spirit had a beautiful singing voice and possessed the gift of mind control. Encantados even had the power to control the weather. On the day of conception, a warm breeze blew through the realm announcing the end of an era.

Chapter 2: The Age of Darkness

The Realm of Lost Souls had formerly been known as the Realm of Forgiveness. It was now a frozen wasteland. Similar to

Alaska in the Winter, the realm was doomed to eternal darkness. Most of its inhabitants lived in shabby, cobbled together huts. The horizon was flat, all except for the castle that housed the Ruler of Darkness. He had arrived like a thief in the night on the back of a golden horse. He was a handsome young man. His bronze, sun-kissed skin accentuated his rugged jawline, and his waist length hair was a ruddy brown. According to him, his hair was locked with the blood of his enemies. He came to warn the realm of impending destruction from a rival dimension. The realm had never been threatened before, and he seemed like the man to protect them. As such, they made him their Ruler. Soon they learned that the only threat to the realm was from the Ruler himself. The longer he ruled, the darker the realm became. Despite the prophecies, the Ruler of Darkness was not to be easily thwarted. He always had a backup plan to maintain his hold on this place.

Before his arrival, this was a flourishing realm. Although it had always been a cold place, the realm was covered in lush greenery. Souls would come here to seek forgiveness and be released to the afterlife, but now souls would come here for torture and mutilation. Everything was either dead or dying. The Ruler of Darkness was proud of the world he had destroyed, and he had no plans on losing it. To maintain status quo, he captured the Sacred Souls as their bellies approached full gestation. The plan was to execute the mothers before the Innocents could take their first breath…but the Universe always provides.

On the night of their 9th full moon, there was a storm. This storm was unlike any other that the realm had experienced. The clouds rolled in, and the Realm of Lost Souls was covered in an impenetrable darkness. Many tried, but there was no light bright enough to illuminate this night. Using the darkness to their advantage, the Sacred Souls escaped. But the longer they ran, the more intense the storm grew. There seemed to be a direct correlation between the ferocity of the storm and the labor pains. The pain forced the Sacred Souls to stop their journey on the edge of the realm. Without light to guide them, they chose to form a circle of protection and deliver the Promised Ones where they had stopped. Their screams echoed through the barren wastelands as they furthered their bloodline; the Coven had grown. The three female babies were born to the realm on the darkest night in its existence, but they alone held the key to the light. As the prophecy promised, the birth of The Innocents marked the end of the darkness, and the storm began to dissipate. When the thunder became faint, and the clouds rolled back to their homes, the sisters ran with their infants. They exited the realm through a crack in the Wall, and The Innocents were never seen again.

Chapter 3: The Hidden

The Sacred Souls knew that The Innocents would never be safe unless they did not exist. The women moved through many realms searching for a safe haven until they found a realm known as Second Earth; Second Earth had always co-existed with the first Earth, just in a parallel dimension. As a result, of war, the first Earth had been destroyed. If only the humans had known how much more the Universe had to offer, then maybe they would not have died over worthless pieces of land.

Second Earth was seemingly identical to the first, except for the Guardians. The League of Guardians had been established centuries before to ensure that Second Earth did not suffer the fate

of the first. The League was made up of Guardian Daemones.

These creatures existed in many forms, none of which would allow

them to move outside of the shadows.

The mothers roamed aimlessly through Second Earth until

they found themselves in a desolate field covered by the full moon.

It was then that they first attempted to seal the wall that led to the

Realm of Lost Souls. Chanting seemed to have placed a temporary

seal, but the sisters knew that it would not last. Their only hope

was to look to an unspoken magic to bind the passageway, but this

magic required sacrifice. Each woman placed a newborn baby on

the ground as an offering to the wall.

I had to pause. What in the hell did this have to do with
me? I walked over to my desk to check the time on my phone.
Though it felt like hours had passed since I'd been home, it had
only been 30 minutes. The concept of time seems to be slipping
away from me. It's 7 o'clock, and I am getting hungry. I thought
about going to the kitchen, but then my mind wandered back to the
book. I'll just finish this chapter and then grab something to eat

from downstairs. Picking up the book, I laid on my back and continued from where I left off:

The woman with the long black hair was known to the realms as Marlena.

I audibly gasped. Marlena is in this book?

Marlena took an Emerald dagger and looked into the eyes of the child that had once lived inside of her with shame. She thrust the dagger into the soft flesh of the baby and dragged the blade from the intersection of its collarbone to the top of its left shoulder.

Involuntarily, my hand found its way to the scar that Kendra swore was my birthmark. I traced the mark from my collarbone to my shoulder, ignoring the obvious, and continued to read.

The middle sister, Venus, had taken her blade and dragged it across the torso of the infant. Simultaneously, the youngest of the three, Safina, pushed her blade into the heart of the child. Before long the women were drenched in blood and the ground shook. The Wall had been sealed but at a high price. Before the blood had dried, the Sacred Souls invoked an ancient spell to transfer the souls of The Innocents into new vessels. Once that task was complete, the women returned to the bodies of the children they had just slain. They carefully wrapped the lifeless bodies in their blood-soaked garments and dredged on, in hopes of finding their way to the Realm of Lost Souls.

Before the Sacred Souls were able to leave Second Earth, they were stopped by The Guardians. Although The Guardians were aware of the prophecy, that prophecy applied to the Realm of Lost Souls, not Second Earth. The Guardians had witnessed the ritual, and they were not pleased. The Sacred Souls explained that the Ruler of Darkness would stop at nothing to kill The Innocents and that this was the only way to protect the children and fulfill the prophecy. The Guardians looked into their souls and saw that the women were telling the truth. An exchange was made between the two houses. The Guardians requested that the Sacred Souls enchant them so that they could take the form of mortals and walk amongst their charges. In exchange, The Guardians swore to protect The Innocents until the end of their days.

I closed the book. Per Marlena, I read the first three chapters and now I was even more confused than before I opened the book. I'm not sure of what kind of fairy tale land Marlena lives in, but I needed to rest. My brain seemed to agree with me because I was asleep before my head even hit the pillow.

CHAPTER 10: REVELATIONS

I couldn't sleep. My dreams were filled with fairy tale creatures and witches. After an hour of tossing and turning, I gave up. I needed to know more.

"Okay, Chapter 4, you've got my full attention," I said aloud as if the book could hear me.

Chapter 4: The Return

When the Sacred Souls returned to the Realm of Lost Souls with the lifeless bodies of The Innocents, the Ruler of Darkness rejoiced. The sisters spun a tale of loyalty that won them favor in the eyes of the Ruler. For a short while, the women lived in peace. The land became fertile, and the darkness began to wane. With much of the prophecy coming true, despite the alleged death of The Innocents, the Ruler became paranoid. He told the women that since they chose to carry the seeds of beasts, then they would also bear him fruit. The Ruler impregnated the women with hopes of yielding offspring powerful enough to defy the prophecy as it was written.

On the night of their 9th full moon, Marlena, Venus, and Safina lay at the Ruler's feet and delivered three sons. Despite their paternity, the women loved their children. Having already lost three children for this realm, they did not want to suffer that pain again.

Marlena's son had her eyes and the sun-kissed skin of his father. Early on, the boy mastered the art of shapeshifting. When he grew older, it was learned that he could also move through time and space. Marlena doted on the boy, which disgusted the Ruler.

Venus' son looked exactly like the Ruler. At first, the Ruler was pleased as he thought this might be his one true heir, but this son had other aspirations. The boy was the fastest runner in the entire realm. He ran so fast that he often went unseen as he moved from place to place. The Ruler had hoped for a son with a mind for war, not the feet of a messenger.

Safina's son was the Ruler's largest disappointment. The boy was been born blind and he was timid, which made him the son the Ruler hated the most. Although he did not have the luxury of sight, he had been given the gift of healing. He could not only heal the sick, but he could also revive the dead.

Though he could not see it, the Ruler had been blessed with three extremely talented boys. This did not matter to the Ruler because nothing about these sons pleased him. He had hoped for the women to bear him warriors. He needed sons that could help him rule the realm, but instead, he was saddled with warlocks.

One night, in a fit of rage, he summoned his sons to his chamber and slaughtered them one by one. As his sons lay on the floor taking their last breaths, he called for the Sacred Souls to show them what he had done. When the women arrived and saw what he had done to their children, they wept. He expressed his frustrations of how weak their children were and that if this is what they produced, then he no longer had any fear of The Innocents. As he spoke, their tears began to dry and the energy in the room became ominous. The women sauntered to the corpses of their fallen sons and covered their faces in the blood of their offspring. An inaudible chant could be heard, but the Ruler was unmoved by their display. The lights in the chamber dimmed as the women's chant grew louder. Within moments, the Ruler felt his blood begin to boil. His whimpers fell on deaf ears as the women continued. The smell of his boiling flesh fueled their chant, and they danced in the chamber until all that was left of the Ruler was a pile of ashes.

But the women's joy was short lived. The boys' corpses began to writhe as their souls were released into the night. The

Realm of Lost Souls was not a place for the innocent to die. Upon death, the young men's' souls belonged to the realm. Like all of the souls that had come here before them, their souls would to be tormented and tortured until they resembled the monsters that roamed this place. The sisters knew of no magic that could reclaim their souls or halt the transformation. For the second time that evening, the women wept. Unwilling to watch the sons they had raised devolve into beasts, the Sacred Souls escaped the realm never to be seen again.

A voice invaded my thoughts, "He was always such a mischievous little boy."

I turned to see Marlena sitting at my desk.

Without looking my way, she continued to speak, "He had the cutest little face you could ever imagine. In fact," she smiled, "he looked a lot like you."

I sat up in my bed, unwilling to acknowledge what she was implying.

She stood and began to pace the room. For the first time in the conversation, she looked in my eyes, "You would never know that he was so handsome, by the way he has turned out."

"Who are you talking about?" I finally built up the courage to ask.

She responded softly, "You know."

"The boy in the story?" I asked, pointing to the book.

She stopped pacing and sat beside me. Neither of us spoke. After sitting in silence and staring at the glittery teal wall across from my bed for a few minutes, she placed her hand over my birthmark, "I'm sorry." was all she said.

The moment the words left her lips, my mind flooded with memories. I saw things I had never seen before, not even in my dreams. I jumped back, running from her touch, and knocked over my lamp in the process. I attempted to bend down and pick the lamp up, but by the time I reached it, the lamp had returned to its place. I turned slowly to face the woman on my bed.

Marlena shrugged, "Perks of being powerful, you should try it."

I shook my head no. I wouldn't be trying anything. But I still needed answers, "How did you do that? What is all this stuff you just put inside of my mind?"

"They are your memories. I figured you would want them back," she said, "Of course you wouldn't remember this, but your brother has visited you once before. You were a bit older. He took those from you then, but thankfully, I was able to get them back before he was able to find you and finish the job."

"Visited me before? Older?" I asked.

She sighed, "Amina, do you know how old you are?"

I shook my head.

"Haven't you ever wondered why you could remember your childhood so vividly?" she asked.

I didn't speak, but I did nod in agreeance.

"It's harder for the human mind to forget something they've experienced so many times before. You would always run back to your childhood whenever you were feeling afraid, so those memories are ingrained in who you are as a person."

I was still confused.

She grabbed my hand, "This is not a dream, Amina, but this is also not your reality. You have already been 16-years-old Amina."

Her words didn't make sense to me, but I entertained her story, "Well then, why am I 16-years-old again? I feel 16-years-old. I look 16-years old!"

"But you are not 16-years-old. I'm really not sure how you got here. When your brother attempted to steal your power this time, I was able to stop him. He collected the memories he could and escaped through a tear in time. So either he pulled you with him, or you jumped?" she was now looking at me as if she was waiting for an answer.

"Or I jumped?" I questioned.

"Yes, Amina. Did you jump?" She hesitated waiting for something to click, but nothing happened. She continued, "Do you remember wishing you were here, in this place again?"

I thought back to the last dream I had before I woke up in this room, "I don't think so. I just remember a beast yelling at me to run until I felt safe. The next morning, I woke up here."

Marlena nodded, "The beast was likely a Guardian. The Memory Thief must have been trying to attack you in a dream. This is all my fault," she dropped her face into her hands, "I should have taken all of your memories back, but I thought if I let him keep one it would send him in circles long enough to get you safe. The scene was filled with so many people that I thought it would take him longer to pick up your trail. I was wrong."

I listened to her words and at this point I decided that this had to be a dream. Nothing she was saying made any sense. I must have fallen asleep reading that creepy book again. Rather than listen to the dream woman talk my ear off, I proceeded to get into the bed and lie under the covers, hoping it would wake me up from this nightmare.

"You are not dreaming, Amina," Marlena informed, peeling the comforter back. She stared at me with loving eyes, "My child, the dreamer," she gently stroked my cheek.

"I am not your child!" I yelled, pulling the comforter back over my head, "I do not want to be a part of this freak show!"

Marlena stopped stroking my cheek and eased back a little before speaking, "It's okay. I know that this will take some time. But I must warn you, time is not on your side. He's coming for you."

I lowered the comforter, revealing only my eyes. I didn't want to engage, but the sincerity in her voice was concerning, "Why does he want me? You're the one that let him die!"

I could see that my accusation hurt her, but I didn't care.

She eventually answered, "You know, there was a time when he wouldn't hurt a fly, but living in the shadows for so long changed him. He thinks your power can set him free." she shifted on the bed.

I couldn't believe I was saying this, "What about The Guardians? If I am truly your daughter and one of The Innocents, then I thought they were supposed to protect me!"

She sighed, "They were protecting you. All this time, you were being hidden by a cloak. I don't know who the cloak was, but this person was a friend of yours. The Guardians would never tell me who it was. They always feared that someone would torture the information out of me and their efforts would have been wasted."

"So then where is my cloak?" I asked.

"Dead," for a moment that was all she said. She began speaking and I could see the concern spreading over her face, "It was the last message I received from the Guardians before we lost contact. Without knowing where the Guardians are or what happened to your cloak, I had to assume the worst. I don't know who to trust. He could be anyone."

I let out a worried sigh.

"The only one that can protect you now is me," Marlena added.

"I don't believe you." I rebutted, "You told me not to trust anyone and now you want me to believe that you are here to protect me from an evil brother that I never knew about?"

She shook her head in disappointment, "Whether you believe me or not, your life is in danger. Think about it, Amina. If I wanted to hurt you, you would be dead by now. I've had ample opportunity to end your life."

I considered what she was saying, and I realized that if any of this was true, then she was right. I had to trust her, "So what should I do?"

She stood up as if she was preparing to leave, "You have to go back to your real time. He is looking for you here, but if you leave now it will take him some time to catch up. Maybe he'll get stuck in this time long enough for me to connect with a Guardian and get you a new cloak."

She sounded so sure, but I was still unclear on what she meant, "What is my real time?"

She was straight to the point, "I've told you already that you are not a 16-year-old girl. Amina, you are a 26-year-old woman. No matter how afraid you are, you have to go back and let me handle your brother for now. You are no match for him in this time period. If he finds you now, he will kill you."

I understood now, but I didn't want to believe her.

She grabbed my hand and squeezed, "I need you to know that when you go to sleep tonight, you won't remember me when you wake up."

I was not okay with that, "Why not?"

"If he can sense a connection between you and me, then he will find you," she answered.

I scoffed, "So you steal memories too, huh? I guess the apple didn't fall too far from the tree."

A smile escaped her lips, "Your sense of humor is still sharp. You'll be fine without me. Besides, I won't take them all, just the memories of me."

"How will I remember that I should be on alert if you aren't there to remind me?" I whined.

She kissed my forehead and handed me the book, "Keep this close and don't tell a soul what you know. Not even your friends! You can't trust anyone now."

I knew she was about to leave, and this may be the last time I ever saw her. Though I had just met her, I knew that I would miss her, "Thanks for warning me, I guess."

"Goodbye, Amina."

I blinked, and she was gone.

I took a seat on my bed, clutching the book in both of my hands. In one day, things had changed so much. As I came to terms with the idea that I was not at all who I thought I was, I could feel the fear creeping into my bones. I hopped up to grab the notebook off of my desk to jot down my thoughts and clear my head. If I was really going to be 26 when I woke up, then maybe I could give myself a little help with a cheat sheet:

Things I learned today

1. I am Amina Wallace, daughter of a witch and a Kitsune. See creepy, old book for an explanation

2. I am actually 26 years old.

3. I apparently have powers. See creepy, old book for an explanation.

4. I have a brother.

5. My brother is an evil entity that is trying to kill me and I have no idea who he is because he can shapeshift.

6. I can't trust my friends because my brother is an evil entity that is trying to kill me and I have no idea who he is because he can shapeshift.

7. I very well may be completely insane.

The woman I had always known to be my mother still hadn't made it home. The hunger pangs were loud and clear, so I ran downstairs to make myself a sandwich. Midway down the steps I began to hear whispering. I stopped in my tracks. The front door was wide open and I could see two shadows from the kitchen.

I tiptoed down a little further and peered around the corner. If I hadn't just witnessed a woman appear and disappear in front of my eyes, then this scene would have blown my mind. Standing in my kitchen was one of the most terrifying things I had ever seen in-person. The thing had the head of a boar and the body of a fawn. Its thick black fur was matted with what appeared to be blood and it's long, straight snout was moist with sweat. I had seen this thing before. This was the creature from the dream that brought me here.

"Did you actually see her leave?" said the booming voice emitting from the giant boar-like creature. It sniffed the air and quickly turned towards my direction. I moved my head in time to avoid its line of sight.

A familiar voice began to speak, but I couldn't place where I had heard this voice before, "No, she came home, but I never saw her leave her bedroom." I listened closer, but I still could not make out the second voice or where it was coming from.

I stepped down further and leaned around the corner to try and see who the creature was speaking with, and the stair let out a slow creak. The boar-like creature immediately turned to face me

"She's here!" he growled. The creature began to charge towards the stairs. Suddenly, wings appeared behind its back in an erect position as if it planned to carry me away.

Though I wanted to get a good look at the person it was talking to, fear told me to run. I ran up the stairs to my room and locked the door behind me. Pushing everything from my desk onto the floor, I dragged the desk in front of the door to serve as a barricade. As an insurance policy, I opened my window to make it look like I may have gone out that way.

The beast began to beat on the door, and I could hear scratching noises. I hurriedly grabbed *The Age of the Innocents* book from my bed and my notebook from the floor. I decided to hide in my closet behind a sea of clothing. I closed my eyes and tried to tune the banging noises out and fall asleep. I needed to be as far away from here as possible, and sleep promised to take me there. I focused all of my energy on falling asleep, and as if in a meditation trance, I felt myself drifting away. I felt myself losing touch with the world around me as I heard the desk slide across the floor and slam into the closet door. The bedroom door let out a loud thud as it swung open.

"She's not here," said the familiar voice. I heard the window lowering.

I tried my best to listen in and focus on the voice, but I was already gone…on the way back to my true reality.

I had always enjoyed playing pretend. I believe that is why I gave myself the name, The Night Prince. The feeling of nobility it gave me was something that always comforted me behind The Wall.

I thought we comforted you behind The Wall.

Their vanity was disgusting. There was a time before the souls that lived within me chose to speak. Before that time, I would pretend. I pretended that I didn't care what my father had done to me. I pretended that I had never truly been born until the day my father slit my throat with the rusty blade. I pretended not to hear his laughter as my warm blood soaked into the ground and I took my final breath. I had pretended for so long that I was sick and tired of pretending. The moment I was set free, I thought that I was done with pretending. Little did I know, I would need to pretend just one more time to see my plan through.

I pretended to be Amina's friend, Charity, until the weak body of the cloak began to deteriorate. I guess a power like mine cannot be contained within a measly human adolescent. The cloak's skin had begun to blister and boil from the inside out and each day I could feel the layers of skin searing off. I knew that I had to make a transfer but this time I had to find someone much more powerful. To capture my new body, I came up with a plan to lure my prey.

I left the remains of the cloak's body near the school where I had found her. In life, she had been as useless as I'd suspected, but I hoped her death would serve its new purpose. I also dumped the body of the cocky human male with her. I left them holding hands with crowns of roses atop their rotting heads. It took no time for the human authorities to find them. The discovery sent the school into a panic, leaving just enough chaos for me to blend in.

Like clockwork, I saw her gliding through the crowd, anxious to see the bodies slain at Chamberlain High. I assumed she would come here to see if one of the bodies belonged to Amina. I hopped from shadow to shadow until I was directly behind her. I wonder if she could feel me near. Would she even remember who I was? Her body stiffened --she knew that I was watching her.

Kill her, Night Prince!

"Are you going to kill me?" she asked, without turning around.

KILL HER! We want her too!

There was nothing they could say to change my mind. I ran my fingers through her hair and whispered in her ear, "I wouldn't harm a hair on your head."

I could smell the blood pumping profusely through her heart and I couldn't contain my smile. I wrapped my arms around her for the first time in forever and all of her memories began to churn inside of me. I pushed all of the early memories to the side for a later date. Once, I found what I was looking for I breathed in her scent.

Maintaining my hold on her body as we drifted through time, I placed a single kiss on her cheek, "Sleep now."

Her head sunk and her eyes closed as she drifted into a wakeless sleep. Death would have to wait to take her. She and I had unfinished business.

CHAPTER 11: THE PARTY

KNOCK, KNOCK, KNOCK

"Amina, are you in there?" someone shouted.

The shouting coupled with the banging on the door interrupted my sleep, and I threw the comforter to the floor.

"I'm coming!" I yelled, hoping it would stop the incessant knocking.

I sat on the side of my bed, my feet barely touching the floor. The pounding in my head caused me to massage my temples gently. Sliding off of the bed, I made my way to the front door. I lifted myself up onto my tip toes and peered through the peephole.

"Why didn't you just use your key?" I grumbled, opening the door.

Tiana stood at the threshold, hands on hips, "Because, I lost it. Why are you still asleep when we have to be at the field with Kendra in like," she glanced at her cell phone, "twenty minutes?"

I headed back towards my room. Tiana followed, closing the front door behind her. For the first time since I had been so rudely awakened, I looked around the room. I noticed that the glittery teal colored walls had been replaced with a more neutral cream color and that my bed had almost doubled in size. No wonder my feet hadn't touched the floor. I looked back at Tiana and it hit me. The attitude was the same, but she was definitely older…and so was I. I had finally woke up from that crazy dream. Out of the corner of my eye, I caught a glimpse of my nightstand and saw that the leather-bound book and my personal notebook were neatly stacked beside my lamp.

It wasn't a dream.

"What day is it Tiana?" I asked, searching for my cell phone.

Tiana plopped on my bed, watching my every move like a hawk, "It's going to be D-day if you don't get dressed. Are you kidding me right now? It's Kendra's annual fall festival!"

She reached under my pillow and handed me my cell phone.

I grabbed it and quickly scanned the text messages, but I couldn't find anything. All the texts asking for help were gone. Wait...

"How did you know I was looking for my cell phone?" I asked hesitantly.

The words *TRUST NO ONE* were echoing in my head.

She shook her head and walked towards my closet, "Because you're always looking for your cell phone. Are you still drunk from last night?"

"Last night?" I questioned.

Tiana was now throwing clothes onto my bed from my closet, "Yeah, last night! We drunk waaay too much wine!" She laughed loudly, "and the prank calling was so crazy that you hid your phone under your pillow!"

My heart skipped a beat when she mentioned prank calling. If the prank calling had happened, then where are the texts?

"What are you doing in my closet?" I asked.

She poked her head back through the closet doorframe and pointed at the bed, "Put those on!"

I picked through the items she had tossed out for me to wear and settled on a simple three-quarter sleeve, black dress. I admired the Bodycon dress in the full-length mirror hanging on my wall. The knit material was hugging me close and I was debating on whether I should wear Spanx or breathe when Tiana emerged from my closet.

"I knew you'd choose that dress," she smiled, smacking my butt as she walked by.

She was wearing low cut denim jeans with a black leather crop top.

"I think you just wanted to dress alike," I teased.

She made her way to my nightstand and ran her hand across the leather-bound book, the same way she had when we were 16-years-old.

"Where did you get this?" she asked, picking it up and thumbing through the first few pages.

I grabbed the book and tucked it in my purse, "I'll tell you about it later. We need to get to Queen Kendra before she sends the SWAT team out for us."

She reached for the book a second time, but I swatted her hand and made a beeline for the front door. I noticed that Tiana wasn't behind me. I walked back in and saw her hovering in my room. She was staring at my bed with a crooked smile and she hadn't even noticed that I had left. After one too many seconds of silence, I grabbed her arm and forced her out of my apartment. I guess there is a first time for everything. I was usually the one being dragged around between Tiana and myself. Plus, she hated being late to anything.

Once we were in the parking lot, I tossed my keys in her direction "Can you drive?"

She had been quiet since we left the apartment, but she nodded affirmatively. She was acting weird, but for all I knew this was the new normal. I sunk into the passenger seat of Tiana's new car. I couldn't help but think about how nice it must be to have older men buying you things all the time.

"When did you get this one?" I questioned, running my hand along the wood grain interior.

She looked over at me and shrugged, "I don't remember."

I fanned myself, "That many of them, huh?"

She clutched the steering wheel and put the car in reverse, "It's not that, Amina. I really just don't remember."

I shook my head. I sensed that she was moments away from being in one of her moods and I did not want to deal with it. For the sake of the remainder of the night, we rode in silence to

Kendra's venue.

"What a strange place?" I said to Tiana as we pulled up to

the field that Kendra's father had shut down for her sweet 27.

"Have we been here before?" Tiana asked looking at me.

The tone of her voice and the look in her eyes let me know she

already knew the answer to the question.

I took in my surroundings. It sure does pay to have an

extremely wealthy, absentee father. The land seemed to go on

forever. I was in awe. The sun was attempting to peek through the

clouds, but the weather promised to stay at a perfect 76 degrees

Fahrenheit. A Kendra Carter event was never too hot or too cold,

and it never rained! Kendra had always been so lucky when it

came to weather.

The more I looked around, the more I felt like I had been

here before. Unfortunately, I couldn't actually recall ever having

been here. That may have largely been in part to Kendra's team

turning the field into a Winter Wonderland in the Fall. I could barely see past the white, sheer canopies that covered the grounds. The canopies were all draped with crystals for effect. If I had to guess, each canopy could hold at least 20 people which would be necessary because Kendra's parties are always packed! A cool breeze greeted Tiana and me as we approached what appeared to be the main tent. As we crossed the threshold, the wind caused the sparse branches above us to shake their remaining leaves to the ground.

"There you two are!" Kendra pouted, waving us into her tent.

Kendra's natural hair was pinned to her head with flexi-rods, and she was walking around in a pink, sequined robe.

"Do you plan on putting on any clothes?" I asked, pulling her into a hug.

Kendra looked frazzled, "I hope so. The stylist is supposed to be picking out my looks, but she has been missing in action for the last 15 minutes." Kendra's voice elevated with each word.

I looked around the tent and my eyes lingered on the racks of clothing that were in the corner of the tent.

"Do you mind if I hide my purse back there?" I asked.

Kendra waved me away and I took that as a yes. I leaned behind the rack with the most clothing and tucked my purse between two over-the-top Showgirl outfits. I laughed at the thought of Kendra walking around with either of those headdresses on.

"She has a very interesting sense of style, huh?" a woman's voice asked.

I turned and shook hands with the woman I inferred to be the stylist. She tucked a strand of long, black hair behind her ear and sifted through the clothing.

"I really like your dress," I shared, "my name is Amina. I'm here to be bossed around too." I pointed at Kendra, "Best friend duties."

The woman in the white dress waved politely, "Nice to meet you Amina."

I watched her as she dug through the remainder of the racks, completely ignoring my presence. Soon, I started to feel awkward staring at this woman while she worked, so I walked off to find the girls. I found Kendra and Tiana whispering to one another in the same spot where I had left them moments before. They stopped speaking when they saw me approaching.

Self-consciously, I rubbed my hand over my belly, "I should have put on the Spanx, huh?"

Kendra sighed, "You look great," she then raised her voice, "I wish my stylist would hurry up so that maybe I could look great too!"

On cue, the stylist appeared with two outfits to choose from.

Tiana elbowed me in the side and whispered, "Don't we know her?"

"I've never met her," I responded, taking a seat next to Tiana. Leave it to Kendra to have a couch in the grass, in the middle of a field, under a tent.

Tiana shifted uncomfortably in her seat, "I've definitely seen her somewhere before."

Tiana's weirdness was starting to rub me the wrong way, so I turned my attention back to Kendra. She had chosen an off-white, fringed, flapper dress for her first look.

"You don't think this is too much, do you?" she asked.

Tiana and I looked at each other and burst into laughter. Kendra was always so self-conscious about being flashy. The only problem with that is that Kendra never did anything that wasn't flashy.

"I think it's perfect!" Tiana chimed.

"Agreed." I seconded.

I rested my head on the back of the couch and I caught the stylist staring at me. Our eyes locked, but she did not look away. The stare-off persisted until Tiana's voice caused me to look away.

"How long before guests arrive?" Tiana asked Kendra.

"In an hour." she responded before disappearing to another end of the tent.

Tiana jumped up, "Perfect!" She ran over to the clothing racks area and moved some things around. She walked back to the sitting area and plopped down beside me. I hadn't noticed the book in her hand until she opened it, "Now you can tell me about this book."

I snatched the book away from her, "Why are you so interested in this book, T?"

She shrugged, "I don't know, it just looks really interesting."

She bit her nails. She only bit her nails when she was lying, but what could she be lying about? I'm tripping. This whole situation has me overly critical. I decided to put my cynicism to the side and be honest with my friend.

"You're right, but interesting is an understatement. You can read it if you want," I offered.

I didn't care if she thought it was crazy because I needed someone to talk to about this stuff. Plus, if she was reading, she wouldn't be talking to me right now which would give me an opportunity to sort through my thoughts.

Tiana gasped and I looked in her direction. So much for sorting through my thoughts.

"Is this legit?" she questioned.

I raised an eyebrow, "What do you mean?"

"These chicks just killed those babies. And the way they killed them kinda hit close to home." she rambled.

Her interest in the book piqued my interest. I sat up, waiting for her to continue.

"You don't think that's weird?" she questioned.

"Do I think what is weird?" I redirected.

"Those kids' deaths. Didn't they remind you of us? And by us, I mean me, you, and Kendra." she said lifting her crop top to reveal her torso.

The dark line across her abdomen was faint but visible.

"You told me that happened when you were five. You said you fell out of a tree," I reminded her.

"I know what I told you, but I thought that sounded cooler than hey check out my birthmark," she confessed.

"Ok fine, but what about Kendra? She doesn't have a birthmark on her chest?"

Tiana tossed that around in her head for a second, "You're right, but she was born with that heart condition. What's it called, uh, a septal defect or whatever? You know, because she has a hole in her heart."

I wasn't sure if Tiana was trying to convince herself or if she was trying to convince me. Now I had come to terms with the idea that I was an Innocent, but I think I would have noticed if my best friends had superpowers --I think.

"I wish." was all I could manage to say. I excused myself from the sitting area and left Tiana to her thoughts. She had her mind made up. I figured if she read the whole story, she would realize that she didn't want to be a character in that crazy book.

"Amina, can you help me?"

The words sent a shiver down my spine. I had visions of the prank calling and the erased text messages before the voice registered as belonging to Kendra. She was standing in front of me with an unzipped dress. I calmed myself down and zipped her in. Before she asked again, I proceeded to help her remove her flexi-rods.

"Have you ever felt invisible, Amina?" Kendra asked, wrapping one of her curls around her index finger.

The cool breeze returned and was now whistling through the tent. I thought about Kendra's question a while before responding. The last two days had pushed me into the spotlight, but before this there were many days that I had gone unseen.

"Plenty of times," I answered, "What about you?"

She stood up and shimmied in her dress causing the fringe to sway around her hips, "More times than you can imagine. But on days like this, I never feel invisible. Everyone is going to see me tonight."

Kendra stared at herself in the mirror, and my peripherals caught the stylist hovering nearby.

"Is everything okay?" the woman in white asked, approaching us at a rapid pace.

Kendra spun around and shot the stylist a look that stopped her in her tracks, "We're fine."

The woman took the hint and left us alone.

"Maybe I should go grab T so she can see how beautiful you look," I suggested. Something about the energy back here made my stomach turn. All of a sudden, I wished that I was closer to the exit of the tent.

Kendra smiled, "Oh, Tiana!" she sung.

I blinked and it seemed like T appeared out of thin air.

With a smile on her face and the book tucked under her arm, Tiana looked at Kendra, "Is it time?"

"I think so," Kendra responded.

Now they were really freaking me out. I had begun easing out of the room when they both looked my way.

"Where are you going Amina? We need to talk to you." Tiana stated, holding her hand out in my direction.

I continued to stumble backward when I bumped into the stylist.

"Amina, is everything okay?" she asked, gripping my wrist.

I tried to pull away, but the stylist's grip was too tight.

"Let go of me!" I yelled as I yanked my arm free. I darted towards the exit of the tent. I was almost out when I looked back. All three of them, Kendra, Tiana, and the stylist, were running behind me. They were closing in, so I sped up. When I turned back to look at the exit, I ran directly into the broad chest of a man. The collision caused me to fall backward again.

"We've got to get out of here!" the male voice commanded. His hand was stretched in my direction.

I looked up and saw that the broad chest and the extended hand belonged to Jonathan. I hesitated, remembering the last time we had seen each other. Against my better judgment, I grabbed his hand. He tossed me over his shoulder like a rag doll, and ran towards his car. When he let me down, I looked up and saw the three women staring at me from the entrance of the tent. I hurriedly jumped into the passenger seat and locked my door.

"Are you okay?" he asked, burning rubber as he pulled out of the parking lot.

I shook my head yes and closed my eyes.

"I'm so glad that you are okay. I thought…well, I thought that something might have happened to you for a second there…."

He continued to babble about how happy he was, but I wasn't really listening. I had closed my eyes hoping to relax a little. I didn't know what was going on with Tiana, Kendra, and her stylist, but I knew I needed to get out of there. I tuned back into Jonathan and he was still blabbering. With my eyes closed, I began to actually listen to his voice. I was immediately hit with another memory. The more he spoke, the clearer it became --this was the voice I had heard talking to the beast when I was hiding in my closet many years ago.

I opened my eyes and stared in Jonathan's direction, "Who are you? I mean, what are you?"

He pulled the car over on the side of the road, "What did you just ask me?"

"I knew I had heard your voice before," I began, "I heard you that night when I was 16-years-old. You were in my house, talking to that monster about me. So, what are you?" I demanded.

He dropped his head and peered over in my direction, "This is not the time, Amina."

I pulled at the door latch in an attempt to escape, but it was locked from the outside.

Releasing the wheel, Jonathan threw his hands in the air, "I go through two time jumps for you and this is the thanks that I get! All you care about is what I am?"

I closed my eyes, expecting the worse, "Please don't hurt me!"

Silence

When I opened my eyes, I was surprised to see Jonathan staring back at me with remorse in his eyes, "I didn't mean to scare you, Amina. But if I tell you what I am, you might not like it."

I braced myself. Was Jonathan my brother?

He exhaled before speaking, "I'm your Guardian."

A wave of relief washed over my body and I finally let go of the door latch, "So you're a good guy?"

He smiled, "Something like that."

I let my guard down and relaxed a little. Once he saw I was no longer freaking out, he started the engine back up and pulled off.

"Where are we going?" I asked after we had been driving for about 30 minutes.

For the second time today my mind screamed, *TRUST NO ONE!*

But it was too late. We were here. The car came to a stop, and the loud screech of the brakes caused me to jump.

Turning off the headlights, he grabbed my hand and squeezed, "You don't have to be afraid anymore Amina. I'm the only one that can help you now."

CHAPTER 12: TRUST NO ONE

We parked in front of what looked to be an abandoned warehouse. The bricks were worn and the windows were all boarded up. Jonathan turned the engine off and stepped out of the car. Walking towards my door, he motioned for me to exit the vehicle. I hesitated as I stared at the man that I thought I knew. I wanted to trust him, but I was afraid.

"We're safe here," he reassured me. He opened my car door and helped me out of the car. As we walked to the entrance of the building, the fear began to creep back into my mind.

"How do you know this place is safe?" I asked.

He smiled at me and pulled me in for a much-needed hug, "Because I would never let anything happen to you." The familiar scent of his cologne was comforting; it reminded me of the times we shared before all of this. I took a deep breath and disregarded the silent alarms going off in my head. I trailed behind him and we made our way into the building.

The emptiness of the building was jarring. It was obvious that no one had inhabited the space for many years and that somewhere along the line it had been gutted. We found ourselves stumbling over forgotten pieces of furniture in the darkness, so he attempted to flick on the lights. The cold, damp smell that lingered in the walls should have been an indication, but we soon learned that there was no electricity in this building. He tilted his head to the side and stared at me.

"So what all do you know about yourself?" he asked, digging into his pockets. He pulled out a match and lit a mostly melted candle that sat on top of a wooden desk that had become a termite's nest. The flame danced and illuminated the room briefly before it fizzled out. The moisture in the air was unforgiving.

I shrugged, "All I know is what the book told me."

My mind raced back to the book that I had left in Tiana's possession and I became angry. That was the one thing I had that could tell me what I needed to know and who I needed to look out for and I left it behind because I was too scared, as usual.

"What book? And is everything ok?" he asked. His teeth chattered as he spoke. I guess the cold was getting to him.

I had hoped that my anger wasn't visible, but it wasn't too shocking that he knew me better than I knew myself. I sighed, "I had this book that could tell me everything about all of this craziness. It told me all about the Innocents, the Guardians, my parents, and my powers." I stopped to take a breath, "I just realized that I left it at the field when I was running away." I slammed my hand on the table and the lights flickered around us, "I needed that book!"

Grabbing my hand, he led me over to what looked like a circuit breaker box, "Did you ever read the part about you having powers?"

I laughed at his peculiar question, "No, it just inferred some stuff early on. But I mean, come on Jonathan, I think I would have known if I had superpowers."

He placed my hand on the breaker box, "Actually, you wouldn't. I'm really good at my job."

The word job made something bubble up inside of me. All of these years he'd been playing me. I was just a job to him. I was sick of being lied to, "And what exactly was your job, Jonathan? Hmmm, make me fall for you and then break my heart over and over again" I asked. The lights flickered again, but just like before the glow only lasted briefly. Before the darkness returned, I could have sworn I saw something move out of the corner of my eye.

He lowered his head and began to speak, causing me to shift my focus, "My job was to keep you safe and to keep you from using your powers. I didn't plan to love you, hell I didn't even plan to like you. My feelings for you had nothing to do with my job. But that is a topic for another day, let's focus on getting out of the dark."

I raised an eyebrow at him wanting to continue the conversation, but the darkness was beginning to make me paranoid. Crossing my arms over my chest with as much sarcasm as I could muster, "And how do you suggest we do that?"

He grabbed my hand and placed it on the circuit box again, "Have you ever noticed that when you are really scared or really upset the lights around you start flickering? Or what about all the static electricity you attract? Come on Amina. You get shocked more than anyone else you know and you've never questioned it."

I was not impressed, "What does that have to do with anything?"

He exhaled impatiently, "Long story short, you are an incredibly talented woman, but one of the more interesting of your talents is your power to control electricity." He scoffed, "I mean, come on, you *are* a Kitsune, Amina. So, could you do us both a favor and hit the lights?" he added jokingly.

I stared at him waiting for a punchline that never came "And here I thought I was the crazy person. Even if I am the female Static Shock, I have no idea how to do any of that stuff."

He placed his hand over mine, "Just think about how pissed you are that you left the book behind or maybe even think of how pissed you are at me. And then you have to focus. Just focus on turning on the lights."

I was skeptical, but what did I have to lose? Closing my eyes, I thought about all the nights I wasted crying over a boy that was just doing his job, and about how weird my friends were acting. I thought about the fact that I couldn't trust anyone and I felt my temperature rising. I tried to imagine the lights coming on, but this was so weird.

With my eyes now closed, I was concentrating harder than I'd ever concentrated before, "I don't think I know what I'm doing," I said.

Jonathan relinquished his grip on my hand that was on the circuit breaker, "You sure about that?"

I opened my eyes and saw that the lights were on in the entire building.

"You have got to be kidding me?" I mumbled. My eyes darted around the room, waiting for someone to jump out and scream 'GOTCHA,' but that did not happen.

He smirked and grabbed my hand again, "I always told you that you are special. Now come on, we need to get out of sight. Terrence is waiting for us."

"Too late," a muffled voice announced from the opposite side of the room.

We looked around. Despite the fact that the lights were all on, we saw no one.

"Who's here? Show yourself!" Jonathan demanded.

The disembodied voice chuckled, "I don't answer to you, beast!"

Jonathan's palm immediately became sweaty.

"What's wrong?" I whispered, looking at Jonathan. He did not turn to face me. Instead, he was staring into the only shaded area of the room. I didn't know what to do, so I stared into the corner as well.

"Do you see me now?" the voice sang.

The voice echoed in my head and I felt like I was having déjà vu, "Who are you? Do I know you?" I shouted.

I felt the grip Jonathan had on my hand loosen, almost as if his hand was yanked from mine. His body jerked backward and slammed against the wall behind us.

The mystery voice lets out a scream of delight and a woman's silhouette could be seen standing in the shadowed corner, "So we meet again, Amina."

She approached. It looked like she was floating rather than walking. As the silhouette of the woman came into focus, I quickly recognized the long black hair. Not to mention, she was still wearing the same white dress from earlier. It was that stylist from Kendra's party. What is she doing here?

"Why did you follow me here?" I asked, backing up towards the wall where Jonathan's motionless body lay. I was too afraid to check if he was still breathing.

My fears were silenced when Jonathan began to shift. He opened his eyes and stared at the stylist, "Marlena?" he said perplexed.

I knew that name--the lady from the book. The woman's face grew dark, and almost immediately I realized that she looked nothing like the stylist from earlier. I mean she looked like her, but at the same time she didn't.

"Wrong again, beast!" she spat.

An evil grin spread across the woman's face and she winked at me. Simultaneously, the sound of light bulbs shattering echoed throughout the empty building. We were in the dark again.

I helped Jonathan to his feet and we ran towards the door, but it was locked from the outside.

"Oh no, sweet Amina, you cannot run from me anymore. This is your destiny!" the woman taunted.

"I know the name Marlena," I whispered to Jonathan. We were crouched beside the door. Clutching onto his hand, I asked, "Isn't she my mother? Why is she trying to kill us?"

He cracked his neck and I saw a fire in his eyes I had never seen before, "That is not your mother."

I was tired of being confused, so I did the only thing I could think to do, "Who are you!" I shouted.

The weight of two hands on my shoulders sent chills down my spine, "You know who I am."

My body's reacted to the voice in my ear and my heart began to race. The stylist's voice had changed. This was now the sinister voice from the prank phone call.

"Sleep now," the voice whispered.

I tried to run, but my body obeyed the command.

⁂

The numbing cold of the ground caused me to shiver and I awoke from a deep sleep. I could not readily tell where I was, but the lingering moisture in the air led me to believe that I was still in the abandoned building. The sound of shattering light bulbs resurfaced in my memory and I shuddered. As I waited for my eyes to adjust to the darkness, I used my hands to familiarize myself with my surroundings. My heart stopped when I felt clammy, cold, human flesh.

"Jonathan?" I whispered.

No response.

I heard movement where the flesh once lay, but I still could not see who was here with me. The silence was excruciating.

"Who's here?" I asked again.

"I won't fall for it again," my unknown companion responded.

"Fall for what?" I probed.

The voice sighed, "Just leave me alone."

"Can you help me?" I asked.

Silence.

"No one can help you here," were the last words I heard for a short while.

It was something about the way this person said the word help that felt familiar. It took me a few seconds before I realized who the voice in the dark was.

"I know you," I said.

The voice let out a reluctant laugh, "No one knows me."

The voice was right, "Well, I don't know exactly who you are, but I do know that I called you one night and you asked for my help, but I couldn't help you either."

Silence.

I continued, "Were you the person texting me? Do you still have the phone? How did we get here?" the questions tumbled out on top of one another.

There was no answer, but I could feel the person's presence moving in my direction. Soon, I could feel their shallow breaths on my shoulder.

"Amina?" the voice asked, "How do I know it's really you?"

The words left my mouth before I even had a chance to think of an answer, "You will just have to trust me, even if you don't trust yourself."

Silence.

"Illuminos Parvu," the voice whispered. A small glimmer of light appeared between us and I was face to face with the person that had started all of this chaos in my life. I jumped back once my eyes registered the face. It was *her*.

"What's wrong?" she asked.

I scooted into a nearby dark corner, "Leave me alone! I don't know what you want, but you need to stay away from me!"

The woman extended her hand in my direction, "You don't have to be afraid of me. What is wrong?"

I stared at her in disbelief, "Is this some sort of sick joke to you?" I shouted, "You bring me here and then you don't understand why I'm afraid? You just tried to kill me! Where is Jonathan?"

The hand that was once extended in my direction was now moving the wisps of hair from her face, "He is parading around as me." She shook her head, "Now you need to trust me…even if you don't trust yourself. I would never try and hurt you. Not to mention, I've been trapped here for longer than you could ever imagine."

I stared at her hand, unwilling to touch this crazy woman. I was sick of playing these games.

"Trust me. I will never hurt you," she goaded.

This was the second time I had heard these words tonight. Each time someone said them, I ended up in an even worse situation than before.

"Where is the phone?" I questioned, ready and willing to do whatever it takes to get out of here.

"There is no phone." she responded calmly.

I shook my head at her, "You want me to trust you, and then you lie about something as trivial as a phone?"

The woman's voice stayed calm, "I never had a phone, Amina. I channeled your electrical signal. I had been trying to reach you for so long and when I finally got through, he heard me. So then I tried just to send words so maybe he wouldn't find you, but he's smarter than even I knew. I was even able to visit you for a brief moment, but that's how he found me," She seemed to be struggling with what she was saying.

"Who is he?"

She extended her hand in my direction again, "Take my hand and I'll show you." The small light caused the shadows to dance on her face and something about her eyes eased my suspicion. I accepted her extended hand.

Her touch sent a jolt of electricity through my body which kick-started a reel of visions. The same types of visions I used to dream about. These were memories. I watched the world through this woman's eyes and I knew that this was the real Marlena and she is my birth mother. What I saw shocked me. According to these memories, we had met many times throughout my life even though I could only remember just meeting her earlier this evening. I would soon get an explanation when I saw her take my memory of her away. The last moment I saw was her standing in the courtyard of my school. She was staring at something on the ground. It looked like a person...wait, a body? I looked closer to see who it could be, but then everything faded to black. The memories were gone.

I dropped her hand and began to fire off questions, "What happened? Who were you looking at? Why didn't you want me to remember you? Why are we here?"

"I thought if you didn't know me then you would be safe, even if I was always close by, but we were betrayed." With her last word, the glimmer of light extinguished.

The loud thuds of two pairs of footsteps approached.

"What a sweet little family reunion." a nasal voice teased.

"I hate family reunions." a second voice chimed in.

The shadow voices laughed amongst themselves before continuing their banter, "How are you little ladies doing today? Turn the light on T!" the nasally voice shouted.

The room was immediately filled with light and I stared in the direction of the two men that had been laughing before. The taller of the two men stepped into the light and I was unable to contain my gasp. His skin was covered in scales and the scales formed the pattern of a copperhead snake. The scaly skin appeared wet, but it wasn't. I know because he knelt beside me and rubbed his hand against my cheek; the skin was as tough as leather.

"Don't touch her! The boss wouldn't like that." the second voice yelled. The bass in the voice forced me to turn my head towards the sound.

"Terrence?" I shuddered as my images of our cordial morning and afternoon chats ran through my mind.

He winked in my direction, "Don't be so surprised little girl, almost everyone you know is a liar!"

My world continued to shatter around me and I simply hung my head in disgust.

Marlena was visibly outraged, "We trusted you!"

The snake-man, still dangerously close to me, whipped his head in her direction and pulled her to her feet by the throat, "No one told you we could be trusted!"

A door swung open from across the room, "Release her!" a new voice shouted.

The scaly creature released his hold on Marlena's throat.

"Sorry, boss," he muttered.

Marlena's body crumpled to the floor, but my attention was still on the new guest in the room. I watched as the late comer walked towards the group. My eyes could not believe what I was seeing. I shut my eyes and opened them again just to be sure.

It was the other Marlena; the Marlena that had thrown Jonathan against a wall.

The other Marlena winked at me again, "Did you miss me?"

I turned to face my birth mother, at least the woman I thought was my birth mother, hoping to get some clarity on what was going on, but she was staring at her mirror image.

"What a waste of power." the other Marlena said, looking in my direction. The imposter crouched low to the ground and the smooth, mahogany skin began to crack like old porcelain. As the pieces of the other Marlena shattered to the ground, a small, deformed figure emerged and stepped over the shell of its previous form.

I immediately moved closer to the real Marlena and buried my face in her hands.

"What a great fucking show!" Terrence spat, clapping his hands, "Can we end this already?"

The creature didn't have a chance to answer.

Marlena wiped my tears and lifted my face before directing her gaze to Terrence, "How could you do this, Terrence?"

Terrence sniggered, "What did you expect Marlena? That we would keep losing our own for the three brats you threw at our feet two decades ago?"

The snake-man joined, "If the people in your realm want them, they can have them! My brother died trying to keep *your* enemies behind that Wall."

"But we had a deal!" Marlena cried out.

"And we made a new deal!" Terrence snapped, "one that wouldn't involve the loss of Guardians for bastard seeds from another realm."

I muttered, "Is Jonathan in on this?"

Terrence rolled his eyes at me, "Is that really all you can think of right now? I will never understand how he could put up with your naiveté."

He didn't answer my question. My heart grew heavy as I considered that Jonathan had set me up.

The deformed creature raised its hand to silence the room With the attention back on him, he began to speak, "Enough of this foolish banter. You know what the problem is with you two," it asked, pointing at Marlena and myself, "you are so trusting. You wanted to believe in the good guys so bad that you didn't even notice they hated you. Do you really think you can count on other people to keep you safe? What a joke! Do you know where trusting people and counting on them landed me? Alone…in the dark…. With no one to count on, but myself!"

"I'm sorry, my son" Marlena whispered.

The monster crept towards Marlena and when he was only inches away from her face, he hissed, "I have not been your son for a very long time."

Marlena did not flinch, "No matter what became of you behind that wall, I will always be your mother." She attempted to touch his cheek, but he slapped her hand away.

I sighed, wondering how my normal life had turned into this nightmare.

"Something wrong, sis?" the creature joked.

"Just kill us already," I stated, ready for this to be over with.

"Kill you?" he smirked, "I wouldn't give you the satisfaction of just killing you. I want you to feel what I felt." He cut his eyes to Marlena, "And I want you to watch...again."

This creature that was apparently my brother slithered towards me. I closed my eyes and my mind drifted to the people I loved that I thought loved me. Kendra, Tiana, and Jonathan flashed in my head. If this was it for me, I wanted to remember them. For once, I was not afraid. When I opened my eyes, I was face to face with the one who was known as The Memory Thief. His mouth opened and revealed blood stained, razor sharp teeth. He dug his nails into my shins and the escaped blood created a trail down my legs. He eyed the blood but continued to claw his way up my body.

"Do you know how long I've waited to bathe in your blood?" he whispered in my ear.

I saw his eyes wander back to the blood that had pooled at my feet and I whimpered when I felt his tongue on my skin. He dragged his tongue from the puncture wounds to my toes with a ravenous fervor. Once he'd had his fill, he wrapped his hands around my neck. Marlena screamed. I noticed that his face or I guess the area that should have been a face, filled with joy at her pain. I was so focused on his face that I hadn't noticed he had released my neck until I felt the sharp nails trace my birthmark. I closed my eyes in preparation. When the nails pierced my flesh, I gasped. The pain forced my eyes open.

I felt the warm gush of blood pour down my chest as the room fell silent.

CHAPTER 13: SWEET DREAMS

"Is everyone okay?" the snake man questioned, dragging the limp body of the memory thief away from my feet.

I had opened my eyes in time to see Jonathan slit The Memory Thief's throat with what appeared to be an Emerald dagger.

"Hurry, we don't have much time!" Marlena shouted as she held the dying monster in her arms. She rocked back and forth, stroking his face with her free hand. She began to whisper the same words over and over again, "Though many spirits be bound to this flesh, may your soul be set free."

I continued to stare in disbelief. What is happening?

"Are you ready Matthius?" Terrence asked.

The snake man whom I will assume is Matthius nodded affirmatively and laid on the ground beside the lifeless body of my brother.

I couldn't sit silently any longer, "What is going on here?" I asked.

For the first time in minutes, everyone looked at me. Jonathan approached and knelt beside me, "I told you I would never let anything happen to you. We knew the Memory Thief had escaped the Wall and we had to lure him into a trap. Everyone is here for you."

Matthius was now lying on his back and he looked over in my direction, "You are our purpose, Amina. The Guardians will always protect The Innocents, even in death."

With those words uttered, Terrence grabbed the emerald dagger that had just been used to kill The Memory Thief and dragged the blade across Matthius' neck. Matthius' eyes never left mine as I watched the light dim in his.

"Marlena, do your thing!" Terrence grunted.

Marlena now sat between the two bodies and placed her palm on the open wounds at their necks, "Metaphora corporis! Ligabis mentis! Recordare tantum Matthius!"

The bodies began to writhe simultaneously. Eventually, The Memory Thief's corpse lay still and Matthius' body continued to convulse.

"Can someone please tell me what is happening?" I begged.

Jonathan grabbed my hand, "Don't worry, we're safe."

I yanked my hand away, "You said that last time, and now two people are dead!"

"Matthius chose to die..." Jonathan murmured, "for you. The Memory Thief's soul would search for you forever, even in death. We have to transform him. We need him to believe he is someone else. This is the only way to keep you and your friends safe."

"Transform him into what?" I questioned.

At that point, Matthius' body stopped moving.

"We just transformed him into Matthius," Jonathan answered.

Matthius was still not moving. Minutes went by before anyone spoke.

"He's just lying there. Did it work?" Terrence asked Marlena.

"Be patient," she warned, "For this to work, we need the two souls to merge. Matthius will need to fight hard to make sure the damned soul remains dormant. The Memory Thief must never find his way out of the darkness."

A cool breeze crept into the room and Matthius' body rose to a seated position. No one dared to say a word.

"What happened to me?" Matthius asked, looking around the room.

"You did it, man!" Terrence smiled pointing at the dead body of The Memory Thief.

Matthius looked at the dead body that lay beside him, "I killed the bastard?" he questioned.

Terrence helped Matthius to his feet, "You freaking killed him!"

Marlena looked at me with silencing eyes. I knew my time for Q&A had come to an end.

"Matthius, let me formally introduce you to Amina," Marlena stated.

I stood to make his acquaintance.

"I wish we could have met under better circumstances," Matthius joked, shaking my hand.

The rough leathery skin felt the same, but something in his eyes was completely different.

"Nice to officially meet you," I managed to mumble.

"What are we doing with the body?" Matthius asked, refocusing on the corpse.

"Burn it," Marlena responded dryly.

Without hesitation, Terrence ran out the door. He returned with a can of gasoline and doused the body. Jonathan lit a match and tossed it. As we stood over the burning body, I couldn't help but stare at the new Matthius. He never looked away. In fact, he watched the body burn until the flames disappeared. Marlena swept the ashes into a velvet bag and tied it around her waist. With that mess cleaned up, everyone proceeded to exit the building.

"Should we head back to the party?" Matthius asked, closing the building's main door behind him.

"How do you know about the party?" I asked, immediately on the defensive again.

Matthius chuckled, "Let me show you."

His body swayed from side to side and I saw the scales disappearing one by one. The once leathery, slimy skin was replaced with smooth, wheat-colored skin. His head was adorned with jet black coils and his eyes were a hazel-green hue. I had seen him before. This was the guy that was in the car with Tiana when I was waiting at the bus stop. He was older now, but he was definitely the same guy.

"Are you--?" I began.

He cut me off, "Yes Amina, I'm Tiana's Guardian."

I looked to the others. They, like myself, knew that this was just The Memory Thief in sheep's clothing. Why would they choose to hide that freak in Tiana's Guardian?

Terrence butted into my thoughts, "And before you get all jumpy again, I'm Kendra's Guardian. There, it's all on the table now. Can we go?"

I locked eyes with Marlena, looking for an answer that would make sense of this mess.

"Let's go," Marlena responded, "We can talk more later, Amina."

Terrence's car was nearby, so he and Matthius rode together. Myself, Marlena, and Jonathan all rode back in Jonathan's car.

We were a few miles away from the field when Marlena broke the silence.

"She'll be safe." Marlena assured me, "As long as you remember to keep what you know a secret! You cannot tell anyone! Especially not Tiana."

I hated this.

"I guess I need to trust you guys, huh." I mocked.

"Who else can you trust?" Jonathan asked, pulling into a parking spot.

We had just beat Terrence and Matthius to the party. Terrence jumped out of the vehicle and made a beeline to Marlena.

"We need to talk," he huffed and pulled her to the side.

I had planned to keep an eye on Matthius, but when I turned around he was gone.

"Let's go find your friends," Jonathan suggested.

I walked into the party with him, but I couldn't stop wondering why Terrence was so adamant about talking to Marlena. And where Matthius had disappeared to? I didn't have time to form any opinions because I saw Kendra and Tiana approaching.

"What happened with you earlier?" Tiana asked.

"Yeah, you ran off like a crazy person," Kendra added.

I looked around to make sure that no one was within earshot, "Did you guys get a chance to read the book?"

Tiana and Kendra looked at one another and burst into laughter.

I raised an eyebrow, "I know that stuff sounds crazy in the book, but it's true and we," I gestured towards all of us, "are the Innocents."

Tiana stifled her giggles long enough to speak, "We know that, Amina."

I was taken aback, "What do you mean, you know?"

Kendra shrugged, "Our Guardians told us years ago. We just couldn't tell you. You weren't ready or some shit like that."

Jonathan chimed in, "It was supposed to be an effort to keep what happened tonight from ever happening. We thought that if you didn't know who you were then he wouldn't be able to tell either."

"What happened tonight? Did something go down after you ran out of here?" Tiana questioned.

I nodded yes, "It's a long story, too long to discuss at Kendra's party."

"Excellent point!" Kendra agreed, "When we saw you with the book, we figured they had told you. Now that you're in on the secret, things are going to get so much cooler from here. Watch this!" she said while pointing at the sky.

The still blackness of the sky was being shattered by pure, white snowflakes. I stuck out my hand to catch a snowflake and the icy cold melted against my warmth. This was real snow!

Kendra gave me a wink, "Just a little gift from my real dad."

"This is crazy," I responded.

"And it only gets crazier from here," Tiana added.

I spent the rest of the night listening to the girls share about their experience and their powers. Terrence had apparently told Kendra who she was one day when she was riding the bus to my house. It was a rainy day and he showed her that she had the power to make the sun come out. Matthius had told Tiana about her powers on a date. It was the same day I had seen them riding together when we were 16. Tiana shared that her way with men was just the tip of the iceberg. Her abilities had allowed her to pick up some other skills along the way.

Jonathan eventually left us to chat. Both Tiana and Kendra admitted that they knew Jonathan was my Guardian all along. They apologized that they hadn't told me. After assuring me that he really did love me, they let me know that the rules said he had to stay away. Apparently, Jonathan hadn't always been my

Guardian. When my original Guardian was killed, he was forced to step in as the next in line. I couldn't help but think that in a perfect world, maybe things could have been different with Jonathan and me.

As we sat and chatted about these things I thought only existed in fairy tales, I saw Matthius wander back into the party. I couldn't take my eyes off of him. I was afraid that if I looked away he would transform into the creature that had just tried to kill me.

He approached our table, "I saw your Winter Wonderland effect out there, Kendra. Good work." Matthius complimented.

"Well, you know a Kendra Carter event must always end with something to talk about." she replied.

He nodded, "Well they are definitely talking about it. People are placing bets on whether it's real or whether you have helicopters dropping icy flakes from the sky."

We all laughed and for the first time in what felt like years, I felt like myself. Like the woman I had always wanted to be-- happy, fun, and powerful.

"T, can I borrow you for a second?" Matthius requested.

Tiana shrugged, "It looks like duty calls. I'll be back."

I was feeling so good that I didn't even watch them as they disappeared around the corner of the tent.

"Having a good time?" Jonathan whispered in my ear, sneaking up behind me.

I threw my arms around his neck and pulled him into a deep, passionate kiss.

"Eww, get a room!" Kendra mocked, walking off.

When we finally came up for air, he stared at me with a lustful smirk, "You are going to get me in trouble, Amina Wallace."

I leaned in closer and gave him a kiss on his neck, "I think I deserve a night of fun, don't you?"

No more words were spoken as he pulled me onto the dance floor. He held me close as we swayed under the stars. Our bodies were so close that it was hard to tell where his black polo ended and my black dress began.

"Don't you think it's weird how warm it is out here, even though it's snowing?" Jonathan asked me, running his free hand down my back.

I pulled away and showed him my hands. The palms of my hands radiated a soft red glow like embers from a dying fire. I had been focused on generating enough electricity to keep us warm and I'm glad to know it was working.

"Just a little something I got from my real dad," I teased, repeating Kendra's statement from earlier.

We continued to dance until the party came to an end. Tiana and Matthius had returned at some point, and they hit the dance floor with us. I couldn't put my finger on it, but they both seemed to be distracted. The night ended much too soon, and I kissed Jonathan goodnight one last time. We promised to see each other tomorrow for lunch. Jonathan and Matthius rode home together and so did Tiana and I. Kendra had to make sure everything was wrapped up on time before she could leave, so she told us she would come by in the morning.

The car ride home was fairly silent. My mind was bouncing all over the place and Tiana seemed to be in another world. We were almost home when a question popped into my head.

"Do you still have the book?" I asked her.

She stuck her arm behind the driver's seat and pulled it from the floor, "Here you go, read up!"

I held the book in my lap, happy to have it back in my hands.

"Have you ever met your real mom?" I asked.

Tiana didn't look at me, "Nope. Kendra hasn't either. We've only ever met Marlena."

"Is she alive?" I asked.

Tiana gripped the steering wheel tighter, "I think so." She quickly changed the subject, "Can I ask you something?"

"Anything," I responded.

"Who was coming after you?"

I had promised to keep the Matthius secret, so I figured I could at least tell her this, "I apparently have, well had, a brother. They called him The Memory Thief."

"Wow, he was your brother? I heard them whispering about him a few times. The Guardians told Kendra and me that our brothers were all dead. I guess yours just slipped through the cracks," she stated.

I couldn't even look in her direction as she spoke. The Guardians had lied to them. I knew that if my brother was alive that there was a good chance, theirs were too. Not to mention, my brother was currently living inside the mind of her Guardian. I couldn't get out of the car fast enough when we pulled up to my apartment. I didn't think I could stay quiet if we kept talking about this. We didn't say much else to one another until we were in bed.

"I'm really happy that we can talk to each other about these things now," Tiana whispered.

"Me too," I said.

I watched her toss and turn for quite some time before I allowed myself to close my eyes. I had never been so afraid to sleep before today. I fought long and hard to stay awake, but eventually, the exhaustion took over.

The dry ground cracked under the pressure of my bare feet. I looked around, but there was not another person in sight. In the distance, I could see a tree covered in fruit. The sight of the juicy nourishment motivated me to walk in the direction of the greenery. The closer I got to the tree, I saw the outline of two people sitting in the shade of its branches. I continued my approach. Soon I could make out that it was a woman and a man under the tree. This did not stop me from walking, in fact, it made me speed up. At last, I was close enough to make out the two figures; it was Tiana and Matthius. Matthius looked over at me and motioned for me to join them. I walked in their direction until I saw that Tiana was not moving. I had not noticed before, but Matthius' hands were covered in blood. He began to lick his fingers one by one, the same way The Memory Thief had licked my leg.

"Welcome to the Realm of Lost Souls, Amina!" he shouted, "See you again soon."

He and Tiana disappeared and the roots of the trees began to shake me by the shoulders.

"Wake up Amina!" a female voice shouted.

I opened my eyes and was glad to see it was just a dream.

"What are you doing here?" I asked.

Marlena was standing in my apartment, but she was not alone. Terrence was here too.

"I told you this was a bad idea," Terrence grumbled, pacing back and forth, "I told you last night that something didn't seem right."

Kendra burst into the room. Her hair was all over the place.

"What are you doing here?" I asked, but no one was listening to me.

"Did you find her?" Marlena asked Kendra in a panicked voice.

"Find who?" I probed.

Again, my question was ignored. Kendra responded to Marlena, "Tiana should be here. She came home with Amina last night."

"That's interesting. I just had the strangest dream about Tiana," I yawned while musing aloud.

This time they heard me. Marlena turned her attention on me, "What was the dream about?"

I thought back, "It was weird. We were in the Realm of Lost Souls which is that place I read about in the book. She and Matthius were sitting under a tree. When I got close, I saw that Matthius was covered in blood, and then they both disappeared. He welcomed me and said see you soon. And then you woke me up. Weird, huh?"

Terrence began to scratch his curly afro, "Jesus fucking Christ!"

"Do you remember her leaving last night?" Marlena quizzed me.

I plopped back into my pillows and shook my head no, "Nope. We both fell asleep here. She's probably in the bathroom, or maybe she went to get coffee. What's going on?"

Terrence answered reluctantly, "We cannot find Tiana or Matthias."

I sat back up in the bed. This was not good. The corner of a pink piece of paper caught my eye from under the pillow Tiana had slept with. I grabbed the paper and saw that it was a note.

"This is Tiana's handwriting," I shared.

Matthius told me that he found my mom. Can you believe it? We're going to some other dimension to meet her, but I'll tell you all about it when I get back.

-Tiana

"If she's with Matthius, then she's okay," Kendra said.

"She doesn't know," I blurted out.

"He found his way out," Marlena said looking at Terrence.

"Who found their way out?" Kendra asked.

Marlena didn't have to answer because I already knew exactly what she meant. The Memory Thief had Tiana and he has taken her to the Realm of Lost Souls.

"We have to go and get her!" I shouted, jumping out of bed.

As soon as my feet hit the floor, all of our phones began to buzz. We had all received the same message:

+Unknown Sender

See you soon.

11:24am

TO BE CONTINUED....

ACKNOWLEDGMENTS

I am so thankful for the unwavering support I received from my mother, Michelle Williams. Mother, you always taught me that I could be anything I wanted to be, so I hope you like having an author for a daughter. I love you very much.

This first installment in this trilogy could not have been completed without the support of Jovan Robinson. Thank you for listening to every idea, every chapter, and every edit. I hope you are ready to do it again (at least two more times). I love you, 500.

Thanks to the girls that have been essential to the development of the person I have grown to be. I hope you can all see your influence on my life via the characters in this story. To Tesia Harrison, Anyia Watson, Ametrice Hunter, Kelly Collins, and Zia Johnson-- I appreciate you all for blessing me with the gift of true friendship.

Finally, I must extend a huge thank you to The Story Detectives team-- Jordan Hayles and Tonesha Sylla! You two lit the fire that led me into the shadows to create this trilogy. I appreciate the early morning/late night phone calls, the guidance, and for teaching me one of my favorite phrases: Absolutely Not.

I'm Writing.

For more information on the series or to sign up for the

Hidden email list, visit:

Facebook: @HiddenFanpage

Website: http://hiddentheseries.com/

Made in the USA
Columbia, SC
26 May 2023

17325706R00152